P9-DOD-834

94-15317

Crider, Bill   18.95
Murder most fowl

OZARKS REGIONAL LIBRARY
217 EAST DICKSON ST.
FAYETTEVILLE, ARKANSAS 72701

GAYLORD M

MURDER
MOST
FOWL

▼

MURDER
MOST
FOWL

BILL CRIDER

94-15317

ST. MARTIN'S PRESS

NEW YORK

OZARKS REGIONAL LIBRARY
217 EAST DICKSON
FAYETTEVILLE, AR 72701

MURDER MOST FOWL. Copyright © 1994 by Bill Crider. All rights reserved. Printed in the United States of America. No part of this book may be used or reproduced in any manner whatsoever without written permission except in the case of brief quotations embodied in critical articles or reviews. For information, address St. Martin's Press, 175 Fifth Avenue, New York, N.Y. 10010.

Library of Congress Cataloging-in-Publication Data

Crider, Bill, 1941–
    Murder most fowl / Bill Crider.
       p.   cm.
    "A Thomas Dunne book."
    ISBN 0-312-11387-0
    I. Title.
    PS3553.R497M87   1994   94–12921
    813'.5411—dc20   CIP

First edition: September 1994

10 9 8 7 6 5 4 3 2 1

FOR LOUISE CARR AND MELVA HARVEY TURNER,
WHO SHOULD ADMIT THAT I NEVER THREW THE DOMINOES

MURDER
MOST
FOWL
▼

1

▼

ELIJAH WARD HAD CHAINED HIMSELF TO THE EXIT DOOR AT Wal-Mart again. It was the second time in the last couple of months.

Ward was about sixty years old. He was six four, and despite his first name he didn't look much like an Old Testament prophet except for the gleam of fanaticism in his dark eyes. He had a red leathery face and black hair with just a touch of gray in it.

Besides about twenty feet of towing chain, he was wearing a pair of faded blue denim pants and a short-sleeved blue shirt that showed the bulging muscles in his upper arms. His unruly hair was only partially covered by a Houston Astros cap.

"You can get in, but you can't get out," Ward told the crowd that had gathered in the glassed-in entranceway.

"That's right," a woman said. It was Ward's wife, Rayjean, who was no more than five feet tall and as thin as a pick handle. She had thin lips and a thin, foxy face. Her thin brown hair was pulled back into a tight bun. "You can get in, but you can't get out!"

She was holding a sign tacked on to a piece of wood that might have been a fence picket at one time. The sign had been printed by hand with a black marker. Whoever had made it had taken the time to do it right:

WAL-MART
Is
UNFAIR TO
THE SMALL-TOWN
MERCHANT!

"They've ruined your downtown," Ward told the curious crowd. "Look at all the empty buildings you've got, nothin' in 'em but pigeon nests. Think of all your neighbors that went broke there, just tryin' to make an honest livin'."

"You can get in," his wife said, waving her sign toward the doors that opened into the store, "but you can't get out!"

No one was trying to get in, however. Everyone was too interested in seeing what would happen to the Wards.

Even the store employees were interested. Most of them had left their positions behind the cash registers and in the departments where they worked to come and see what all the commotion was about. They were all wearing their blue Wal-Mart vests, and they stood just inside the closed glass doors, looking out at the crowd and at the Wards.

Elijah Ward rattled his chains. "You can get in, but—"

"—you can't get out!" Rayjean said.

"You can get in, but—"

"They can get out through the back door in the automotive department," Sheriff Dan Rhodes said, as the crowd made way for him. "Or the manager will just let them out through the 'in' doors, the way he did the last time you tried this."

"Maybe so," Ward said, unconcerned about Rhodes's intervention. "But if they come through the front, they'll have to duck down under that little bar they've got across there to keep people from sneakin' out that way. Got 'em a guard there, too, that they call a 'greeter.' Guard is more like it. They don't trust folks like I did, back when I had a store."

"Things aren't like the way they were then," Rhodes said. "They sure aren't," Ward agreed. "You might as well leave me alone, Sheriff. I'm not leavin' this time. I'm willin' to go to jail for my beliefs."

"Me, too," Rayjean said, pumping her sign up and down. "Take me to the pokey, Sheriff. That's the only way you'll get me out of here."

She was probably serious, Rhodes thought. The last time this had happened, he had been able to talk the Wards into going home peacefully. It looked as if this time it might turn out to be different.

"People don't realize what this store's done to Clearview," Ward said, shaking the chain, which clinked against the glass of the door. "They think it's just a good place to buy things on the cheap, and they don't think about all those empty downtown buildin's where stores used to be."

As Rhodes was well aware, one of those empty buildings had been occupied by Ward's hardware store, but after ten years of trying to compete with discount prices, Ward had been forced to close his doors. While his profits had declined, along with those of the two clothing stores, the drugstore, and the five-and-dime, he had watched a steady stream of his former customers driving to the big new Wal-Mart on the outskirts of town.

"It's competition," Rhodes told him. "It's the American way."

"Not the way the big boys do it," Ward said. "The way they do it, there wasn't any way I could compete with 'em."

There was a bit of mumbling in the crowd, and Rhodes wondered if some of them were beginning to agree with Ward. Ward seemed to think so, and he followed up his advantage.

"They've run us small merchants out of business," he

said. "And now they've got it all." He looked around at the crowd. "Look there. There's Willard Ames. You oughta be ashamed of yourself, Willard, comin' out here. Your daddy traded with me from the time I first opened up. Bought all his fishin' rods from me. Lures, too."

Ames was a young man in his early twenties, and he looked down at the floor as he spoke. "Well, you don't have a store anymore, Mr. Ward. And I needed me a light fixture."

"You'll get it, too," said a man at Rhodes's back. It was the Wal-Mart manager, Hal Keene, a nervous-looking man with a fringe of graying hair and a potbelly. He was carrying a pair of bolt cutters that he handed to Rhodes. "Here, Sheriff. You cut that chain and arrest that man."

Rhodes took the bolt cutters, feeling vaguely guilty. He'd bought a lot of Old Roy dog food at Wal-Mart. Maybe he'd contributed to Ward's delinquency.

"You won't be able to cut this chain," Ward said, rattling it. "It's not that cheesy Japanese stuff that you can cut with a dinner knife. It's a good American chain, left over from my store."

Rhodes walked to the door handle and applied the cutters to a link of chain. He pressed down on the long handles and sheared through the chain.

"Looks like that good old American chain won't stand up to a solid pair of bolt cutters," the manager said. He looked around at the crowd. "Made right here in the U.S. of A. We've got 'em for sale in our hardware department."

Rhodes started to unthread the chain from the door handles. "I'm going to have to take you to the jail," he told Ward.

"That's just all right with me," Ward said. "I told you I was willin' to go."

"What's the charge?" Rayjean demanded, menacing Rhodes with the sign. "Since when is it a crime to stand up for what's right?"

"You'll have to come, too," Rhodes told her.

Rayjean drew back the sign. "You bet I will. That way we can *both* sue you for false arrest."

"I'm takin' my chain with me," Ward said. "You can't take my chain away from me."

"I'll have to confiscate it," Rhodes said, gathering it up. "It's evidence." He looked at Ward. "Are you coming?"

"I guess," Ward said. "Come on, Rayjean."

The two of them walked ahead of Rhodes out to the county car. Some of the crowd trailed along behind, while others went on into the store to get their light fixtures or bolt cutters or whatever it was they thought they needed.

Rhodes put the chain in the trunk of the car. Then he took Rayjean's sign and put it in there as well. After that, he got the Wards seated in the back and closed the doors.

Before he got into the car himself, Rhodes turned to say a few words to the people who had come out of the store to watch.

"You can all go on back inside," he said. "Nothing else is going to happen here."

Hal Keene was standing in the door to the entranceway. "We've got a special on Sam's Cola," he told the crowd. "You'll need to stock up on it for the hot summer days that're coming up."

The word "special" worked like magic and, forgetting about the Wards, the rest of the crowd turned back toward the store, everyone eager to get a good deal on Sam's Cola.

"I'd like to talk to you a minute," Rhodes told Keene as the manager started to follow the crowd back inside.

"What?" Keene said. "You want me to go down and swear out a complaint? I'll be glad to."

"I'd just as soon you didn't," Rhodes said. "What I want you to do is take the outside handles off those exit doors, like I told you to the last time Lige did this. You don't need handles there, anyway."

Keene looked miffed. "He'd just chain himself to the entrance doors if I did that."

"Maybe not," Rhodes said. "I'll have a little talk with him."

Keene pulled a handkerchief out of his back pants pocket and wiped his face and the top of his head. "Lot of good that'll do."

"We'll see," Rhodes said.

He left Keene and went back to the car. When he got in, he turned to the Wards, speaking to them through the screen that separated the front and back seats. "Disturbing the peace, creating a nuisance—"

"What're you talkin' about?" Ward said.

"The charges," Rhodes told him. "You asked about the charges."

"No, he didn't," Rayjean said. "I did. Anyway, those things are just picky little misdemeanors. You can't keep us in jail for 'em."

She was right, so Rhodes didn't bother to answer her. He started the engine and turned on the air conditioner. The cool air hit him in the face, drying the sweat. He put the car in gear.

"Wait a second, Sheriff," Ward said before the car got rolling.

Rhodes turned in the seat. "What's the matter?"

"Look at the parking lot," Ward said. "Not a vacant parkin' space in sight. People so thick you couldn't stir 'em with a stick."

Rhodes admitted that the lot was crowded.

"Now look over there at that grocery store," Ward said. "Covered up, right?"

The supermarket was almost as crowded as the discount store. There was hardly a vacant space in its parking lot, either.

"Remember what it used to be like downtown on a Saturday?" Ward asked. "Two big grocery stores, the A & P and a Safeway, both of 'em doin' a land-office business, with the Piggly Wiggly goin' strong too. Not to mention the mom-and-pop stores all over town. How many of those are left?" Rayjean didn't give Rhodes time to answer. "Just one," she said. "Where the Safeway used to be, but it's an H.E.B. now. All those little stores, there's not a one of them left."

"That's right," Ward said. "And you remember Duke and Ayres and Perry Brothers? Gone. And the JC Penney? That's gone, too, just a vacant buildin' there in the middle of the block. There were four drugstores, but there's just one of 'em left. And the Western Auto's gone. Used to be, you could hardly walk on the sidewalks downtown on a Saturday, but you go down there now, there won't be a single soul. They're all out here at the Wal-Mart."

"And what about that preacher?" Rayjean asked. "The one that used to set up on the corner downtown and set that speaker out on his car hood and preach all afternoon. You think anybody'd listen to him if he set up out here?"

"Probably not," Rhodes said. He wasn't too sure that anyone had listened to the preacher even in the old days.

"The world's changed," Ward said. "And it ain't changed for the better, you can bet on that. There's not any downtowns anymore. There's not anywhere that you can go and walk around and see your friends. There's not any-where a man can set up a small business and sell to his neighbors. The big boys have put a stop to all that."

"Maybe so," Rhodes said, "and maybe it's not all for the good. But that doesn't mean you can go chaining yourself to the doors and try to drive away the customers."

Ward sighed. "I guess you're right about that. I guess we can't ever go back to the way it was."

"No," Rhodes said. "We can't."

"It's a damn shame, though," Ward said. "Don't you think it's a damn shame, Sheriff?"

8

It was a good question, and Rhodes was sorry that he didn't have an answer for it. He backed the car up and drove out of the parking lot.

"I don't see why you just let 'em go like that," Hack Jensen said. He was the dispatcher for the Blacklin County Sheriff's Department, and he liked to have a say in the way things were done. Seeing the Wards get off with a visit to the justice of the peace and a fine didn't sit right. "That Lige Ward's been nothin' but trouble since he closed his store. He oughta get himself a job. That way he'd have somethin' to do instead of causin' problems for other folks."

Hack had a point, Rhodes thought. Not only had Ward chained himself to the Wal-Mart doors twice now, he'd been in a fight at the Palm Club one Saturday night, and Rhodes had gone out to Ward's place in the country twice, responding to complaints by Ward's neighbor, Press Yardley.

"Hack's right," Lawton said. Lawton was the county jailer, and Rhodes knew he was in trouble as soon as Lawton took Hack's part. Most of the time, the two old men didn't agree on anything. "Lige is headin' for trouble."

Hack nodded. "You better listen to what we're tellin' you, Sheriff."

Lawton leaned his broom against the wall. "Yep. If you don't do somethin' about Lige now, he's gonna get in some real trouble later on, if he's not already."

"Do you know something I don't know?" Rhodes asked.

"Hah," Hack snorted. "Don't we always?"

"Like what?" Rhodes said. He was genuinely curious. Though Hack and Lawton seemed to spend their lives in the jail, they actually got around more than Rhodes did, and they often heard things that people wouldn't tell the local sheriff.

"Well," Hack said, "like this here computer." He looked

fondly at the monitor and the big gray box it sat on. "I kept tellin' you for years that we needed one, but you wouldn't listen. You were just like Lige, tryin' to keep on livin' in the past. I was right, though. You—"

"He's not talkin' about any computer," Lawton said. He was no more fond of the computer than Rhodes was. He was past seventy, but with his round, unlined face he looked like a slightly overage cherub. "He's talkin' about important stuff. Like Lige Ward."

That was more like it, Rhodes thought. "That's who I was talking about, all right," he said.

"I'm not the one implied that I knew anything about Lige," Hack said, looking hurt. "And I bet Lawton don't know anything, either. He just likes to run his mouth."

"I've heard a few things," Lawton said. "When you don't spend all your time hangin' out with wild women, you hear a few things."

"You take that back," Hack said, standing up. He was as old as Lawton, but he was tall and thin, with a thin brown mustache. "Miz McGee ain't no wild woman."

Now that things were back to normal, Rhodes relaxed. "If you two can quit jawing at each other, maybe one of you could tell me what it is you know about Lige Ward."

Hack sat down. "I can't tell you a thing. I spend all my time hangin' out with wild women. You'll just have to ask Lawton. He's just jealous, anyhow."

"I ain't jealous," Lawton said. "I don't care how you spend your time. It don't mean a thing to me."

"Never mind that," Rhodes said. "Tell me what you've heard about Lige."

Lawton got a thoughtful look on his face. Rhodes waited expectantly, while Hack looked at his computer monitor as if maybe there was something there in the glowing letters that Rhodes couldn't read from across the room.

"I can't remember," Lawton said after a minute.

Hack laughed. "I may be runnin' with wild women, but at least I ain't lost my mind yet. You've got oldtimer's disease, Lawton, that's what you've got."

It was Lawton's turn to have his feelings hurt. "Don't neither. I know I heard somethin'. I just can't think of it right now." He looked over at Rhodes. "But it'll come to me sooner or later."

Rhodes nodded. "You let me know when you think of it."

"Seems like it had somethin' to do with chickens," Lawton said.

But he didn't think of what he'd heard until a few days later, and by then Rhodes had pretty much forgotten about the whole thing.

It all came back to him, though.

2

RHODES GOT THE CALL ON SUNDAY AFTERNOON WHEN HE AND Ivy were watching Randolph Scott, a particular favorite of Rhodes's, on videotape. One of Ted Turner's cable channels had run six or seven of Scott's movies back to back, and Rhodes had recorded as many of them as he could get on a single tape. The one they were watching was *Decision at Sundown*.

"I never believed those rumors," Ivy said, taking a handful of the air-popped corn from the bowl on the coffee table.

Rhodes took a handful too. He preferred his popcorn soaked with butter and heavily salted, but Ivy insisted that there was far too much fat in such a concoction. So he settled for what he could get.

"What rumors?" he asked.

"You know," Ivy said. "The ones about Randolph Scott."

Rhodes had never heard any rumors about Randolph Scott. He asked again, "What rumors?"

Ivy shook her head, making her short hair dance. "Oh, you know. The rumors that he was gay."

Rhodes sat up straight, nearly choking on his popcorn and forgetting all about the movie. "What?"

"Well, you know. He was rooming with Cary Grant, and there was that photo of the two of them, and Grant was wearing a woman's dressing gown . . ."

"You're making this up," Rhodes said.

Ivy laughed. "No, I'm not. It's all true. I heard those rumors when I was in high school."

"Well, I didn't," Rhodes said. "And I don't believe them."

"Me neither," Ivy said.

The phone rang then, and Rhodes was just as glad. Somehow he didn't feel like watching TV anymore. Not that it made a bit of difference, even if Randolph Scott *had* been gay, which Rhodes didn't believe for a minute, but still . . .

"Hello," he said.

"Sheriff?" It was Hack. "I wouldn't bother you, but Ruth's down at Thurston, and we got a little trouble you need to know about."

Ruth was Deputy Ruth Grady. Even with her out of town, Rhodes knew Hack wouldn't ordinarily call him at home on a Sunday afternoon if there weren't some sort of emergency.

"What is it?" he asked.

"Got a call from down toward Sand Creek. Seems like there's some shootin' goin' on."

"What kind of shooting?"

"Didn't say. Prob'ly just some kids hoo-rawin' around. But there's a baptizin' in the creek today, and the shootin's coming from pretty near that shallow place that Brother Alton likes to use."

"I'm on the way," Rhodes said.

Sand Creek was about a mile out of Clearview, and it was running just about full owing to the heavy rains at the end of May a week earlier, probably the last good rains before fall. The conditions weren't the best for a baptizing, but the place that Brother Alton Downey of the Free Will Church of the Lord Jesus liked to use was about as safe as any. The bank sloped gently there, and even when the creek was full, a man could pretty well immerse someone without getting out in the creek to where there was enough of a current to cause a problem.

Rhodes pulled off to the side of the county road and parked his car as close as he could to the wooden bridge that spanned the creek. There were several other cars already parked there, all of them belonging to the members of Brother Alton's church. Brother Alton's old black Cadillac Fleetwood was in front of all the others.

As soon as he opened his car door, Rhodes could hear gunshots.

He could see where they were coming from, too. There were three young men stumbling awkwardly along the creek bank, and every time there was a clearing in the trees that lined the bank, the men stopped. One of the men would steady his right hand with his left and fire a shot or two through the opening in the trees, and all three men would jump and yell. Then the man who had fired the pistol would hand it to one of the others, who would take his turn at the next clearing.

They were shooting at a portable toilet that was floating right down the middle of the creek.

It looked to Rhodes a little bit like a silver bullet with its base submerged in the water. There were silver grilles around the top near the roof, and there was some lettering on one side, but Rhodes couldn't make it out.

What he could make out was the consternation on the faces of Brother Alton and those members of his small congregation who had gathered for the baptizing. They were standing calf-deep in the muddy water of the creek, hearing gunshots and looking at the silver outhouse that was about seventy yards away and bearing down on them.

Rhodes walked down to the creek bank through the tall

green weeds and grass. There were quite a few pairs of shoes lined up just at the edge of the grass.

"You about finished with your business, Brother Alton?" Rhodes asked.

Brother Alton was tall and thin, and he had on a black suit, a white shirt, and a wide black tie. His pant legs were rolled up to his knees, but they were wet anyway. He wore rimless glasses that reflected the sunlight, and his face was crosshatched with wrinkles.

"It's the Lord's business we're doin' here," he said. "And I'm not so sure we'll be able to finish it. Sister Midgie is mighty upset with all the shootin', and we can't get her completely immersed. You know a baptizin's no good if you're not completely immersed."

Sister Midgie looked at Rhodes miserably. Her hair hung wet and lank, water dripping off the ends of her bangs and running down her face. Her clothes were thoroughly soaked. It appeared that there had been several unsuccessful attempts at complete immersion.

"I'll put a stop to the shooting," Rhodes said. "But I'm not sure what I can do about the toilet."

Brother Alton's lip curled at the mention of the toilet. Rhodes supposed that it was all right to talk about gunshots at a baptism, but portable toilets were something else entirely. Rhodes decided to get back to a more tasteful topic.

"You just relax, Sister Midgie," he said, "and go on and get baptized so you can get out of that water."

"I'll try, Sheriff," Sister Midgie said.

"Good," Rhodes said. "You go ahead with your ceremony, Brother Alton, and I'll go see about those boys with the pistol."

"Drunks," Brother Alton said, drawing himself up self-righteously. "Slaves of the Demon Rum, and on the Sabbath Day, at that."

It was more likely the Demon Lone Star Beer than the Demon Rum, Rhodes thought, but there was no use in getting into a theological argument with Brother Alton. Rhodes started walking through the deep weeds toward the three men with the gun. His feet squished occasionally on the still-soaked ground.

After he had covered about ten yards he looked back over his shoulder. Brother Alton had his thumb and forefinger clasped over Sister Midgie's nose, the palm of his hand covering her mouth. All of her below her shoulders was submerged, and she was sinking fast. Rhodes figured that this time the baptism would be completed. All he had to worry about was three drunks with a pistol.

They saw him coming and started passing the pistol from one to the other, laughing loudly all the while. When he got up to them, the pistol was nowhere to be seen. He didn't know any of them, but they knew him. Or at least they knew who he was.

"Heighdy, Sheriff," they said, almost in unison. A heady odor of beer fumes surrounded them. The three men had probably consumed enough beer to immerse Sister Midgie completely.

"Where's the gun, fellas?" Rhodes asked, looking them over. They were all dressed in western straw hats, western shirts, boots, and jeans, and not one of them was more than twenty-five.

One of them laughed. "What gun?" he asked. He looked a little older than the other two and he had a strong, square chin. "We don't have any gun."

"Sure you do," Rhodes said. "You were using it to shoot up that toilet there." He pointed through the trees at the silver shape floating lazily down the creek.

The three young men broke up in laughter when they looked at the toilet, slapping shoulders and punching arms.

"I don't guess you'd know a thing about how that toilet got there, would you?" Rhodes asked.

That impressed them as being even funnier, and Rhodes thought for a second that they might all fall down from laughing. Before they did, he told them that he wanted them to do something for him.

"Just some simple tests," he said, and told them what he wanted them to do.

They tried, but none of them could quite touch his nose after first closing his eyes, and none of them could quite stand on one foot for more than three seconds. One of them fell over and had to be helped up by his friends, who seemed to think it was one of the funniest things that had ever happened, even more hilarious than Rhodes's mention of the outhouse.

"Where's your car parked?" Rhodes asked after they were all standing and the laughter had subsided.

"Truck," the oldest one said. "We came in a truck."

"Let's go have a look at it," Rhodes said. "The walk will do you good."

Brother Alton had been right. They'd been drinking for sure, and more than a little. Rhodes thought he'd find the hard evidence in their truck. He started walking.

They didn't give him any argument; they just followed along behind him, occasionally stumbling into one another and guffawing.

It was about a half mile to the county road where they'd parked, near a bridge that was a lot more rickety than the one where Rhodes had stopped. On the way there they passed three empty aluminum beer cans. He had the men pick them up.

"They're bringing about thirty cents a pound," Rhodes pointed out. "Besides, you don't want to mess up the environment."

"We didn't put those cans here," the spokesman said.

"Maybe not," Rhodes agreed, looking at the can the man was holding.

It wasn't Lone Star after all. It was Coors Light. The Silver Bullet.

Well, Rhodes thought, you can't be right about everything. Anyway, considering what the outhouse looked like, what could be more appropriate?

When they reached the road, the men were a little more sober than they'd been when the walk had started, but not much.

It was no wonder. There was a red Toyota pickup parked by the bridge. It was backed up to the side of the bridge, so that something heavy, like a portable toilet, could have been slid out and into the creek.

The pickup's tailgate was open, and the truck bed was littered with Coors Light cans, even more than Rhodes had expected. The drinking had been going on for quite a while. Many of the cans were partially flattened, probably from the outhouse's having rested on them. There were sticks and dry leaves and chicken feathers mixed in among the cans near the cab of the truck.

Rhodes walked behind the truck and closed the tailgate. He noticed that the TO and TA had been painted out, so that the tailgate no longer announced the manufacturer's name. It just said, "YO." The tailgate was hot from the sun, and Rhodes moved his hands.

"You can throw those cans you're holding in there with the rest of them," Rhodes said, and they did. The cans clattered against the bed, bounced a time or two and then were still.

"Now then," Rhodes said, "let's take care of a little unfinished business. Where's the pistol?"

One of the younger men, who had ears that stuck out from the sides of his head, said, "He's got it."

He pointed to their spokesman, who didn't say anything. He just reached behind his back and pulled the gun from under his shirt.

Rhodes took it from him. "That's good," he said.

The pistol was a .38-caliber Smith & Wesson revolver. Rhodes opened the cylinder, but there were no cartridges inside. That was even better.

"Now," he told the three men, "let's see some identification."

They got out their wallets and showed him their drivers' licenses.

The oldest one was Michael Ferrin, age twenty-five. The one with the big ears was Kyle Foster, twenty-three. The one who still hadn't said a word was Lawrence Galloway, also twenty-three.

"Well now," Rhodes said, "which one of you wants to tell me how that portable toilet got in the creek? How about you, Lawrence?"

Lawrence blinked. "Larry," he said. "Ever'body calls me Larry."

"All right, Larry. How about it?"

"I guess that was our fault," Larry said, looking down at his dusty boots. "We sorta put it there."

"I figured that," Rhodes said. "The question is, how are you going to get it out?"

The three men looked at one another. No one seemed to have any idea until Ferrin said, "We can rope it."

"Right," Foster said. "That's what we can do. Where's that lariat rope?"

"In the truck," Ferrin said.

Rhodes couldn't think of anything better to do. "Get it," he said.

Ferrin opened the door on the driver's side and pulled the seat forward. He reached behind it and came out with a coiled rope. He slammed the door.

"Here it is," he said. "We can rope that son of a bitch."

Rhodes wasn't sure that any one of the three was in any kind of shape to rope a tree stump, much less the toilet, but at the same time he thought it might be a good idea to try to get it out of the creek before it floated into the next county. It was worth a try.

"All right," he said. "We'll walk back down to the other bridge. There's a good clear space just before you get there, and maybe you can get a rope on that thing from the bank."

"Why do we have to walk?" Larry Galloway asked. "Why can't we go in the truck?"

"Because you need a little fresh air," Rhodes said. "And because you don't want a DWI on your record."

"I'm not intos—intos—in*tox*icated," Galloway informed him. "And I wouldn't be drivin' anyhow. It's not my truck."

"It's mine," Ferrin said.

"I don't care whose truck it is," Rhodes told them. "We're going to walk."

They started back toward the spot where the baptizing was going on. Rhodes could hear Brother Alton's small congregation singing "Shall We Gather at the River," so he supposed the ceremony was over. Maybe they would be gone by the time the outhouse and the ropers arrived.

They weren't gone, however. They had walked back to their cars, but they all stood there watching, waiting to see what Rhodes was going to do. Even Midgie, towels wrapped around her now, was standing there to see what would happen.

What happened was that Michael Ferrin tried to twirl a noose into the rope and got so tangled up in it that Rhodes had to free him. The other two were laughing too much to be of any help.

"I thought you were a roper," Kyle Foster said when he got his breath back.

Rhodes thought that someone had better be a roper or it was going to be too late. The portable toilet was already directly in front of them, and in a minute or two it would be on down the creek and behind the cover of the trees again.

"Give me that rope," he said, and Ferrin handed it to him.

Rhodes had never harbored any illusions about his abilities as a rodeo cowboy, but when he was young he had read a biography of Will Rogers and for a few weeks afterward had spent a lot of hours in his backyard trying to learn a few simple rope tricks. He'd never gotten very good at any of them, but he'd also spent some time lassoing his parents' lawn chairs, and he'd gotten fairly good at that. That had been a long time ago, however. Maybe it was like riding a bicycle and would all come back to him. He hoped so.

He spun the noose above his head, letting the rope out gradually through the loop. When he judged things were about right, he looked at the toilet, which was about ten yards offshore, and let the noose fly.

It flattened out and settled over the outhouse as if Rhodes had been doing that sort of thing every day for years. The members of Brother Alton's congregation applauded.

Rhodes pulled the rope tight, trying to look casual. Then he handed the rope to Ferrin. "You three can pull it in now that I've done the hard part."

The three young men didn't look especially happy about having to do any physical labor, but they pulled on the rope and after a little struggling they had the silver metal building lying on its side on the bank of the creek. There were a number of bullet holes in the sides. There was a peculiarly unpleasant odor about it, but Rhodes supposed that was to be expected. It was a toilet, after all.

He could read the lettering now. It said, SANI-CAN INC. CALL 555-4545."

"Where did you say you got this thing?" Rhodes asked.

"We didn't say," Foster told him, and they all three laughed at his wit.

"My mistake," Rhodes said. "Where did you get it?"

The men looked at one another, no longer laughing. Finally Ferrin said, "We don't exactly know."

"Why not?"

"Well, we were just ridin' around, you know? And we saw this thing shinin' in the sun, and somebody thought it'd be a good idea to take it. But I don't remember exactly where we were when we found it."

The other two didn't remember either. They looked at the ground and shook their heads when Rhodes asked them.

"All right," he said. "You saw it shining in the sun. Then what?"

Ferrin said, "We stopped and put it in the truck. Somebody said it'd be fun to throw it in the creek and see if it'd float."

Rhodes had an idea who the "somebody" was, but he didn't say so. "It floated, all right. Whose idea was the pistol?"

Nobody said anything, but Rhodes had a pretty good idea about that one, too.

"Well," he said, "I guess we'd better be going into town. The county car's right up that way." He pointed in the direction of the road.

"What about my truck?" Ferrin asked.

"I'll send somebody for it," Rhodes said. "You're not in any condition to be driving."

Ferrin opened his mouth and looked as if he might argue, but all he said was, "Well, what about my rope?"

The portable toilet was lying on the rope. Rhodes supposed they could lift it up and remove the rope, but he didn't see any need to do that now.

"I'll have someone put it in the truck later," he said.

Ferrin obviously didn't like that idea. "It's a real good rope," he said.

"Don't worry. Nobody's going to steal it."

Once again, Ferrin looked as if he might argue, but he didn't. He turned toward the road, where the members of Brother Alton's congregation were getting into their cars.

"Let's go," Ferrin said to his buddies.

Rhodes started after them, but there was something about the odor hanging about the toilet that was bothering him.

"Wait a minute," he said.

The three men turned back to him, and he walked over to the toilet. The door was facing him, with the handle about on a level with his belt buckle. The toilet was not completely out of the water, but Rhodes could reach the door handle without getting his feet wet. Just muddy, but then they were muddy already. He thought he'd better have a look and see if there was anything inside the toilet.

Rhodes pulled the handle and the door fell open, slapping into the wet earth of the bank.

There was something inside, all right.

Or, to be more accurate, there was some*one* inside.

It was a big man wearing faded jeans and a blue work shirt. Between his feet there was a Houston Astros cap, the same one he'd been wearing at Wal-Mart.

It was Lige Ward, and he was dead as a hammer.

3

▼

THE DEAD MAN CHANGED THINGS. SUDDENLY MICHAEL FER-
rin, Kyle Foster, and Lawrence Galloway were practically
sober.

"What—who's that?" Galloway said. His face had
turned slightly green. "Is he . . . ?"

"He's dead, all right," Rhodes said.

Galloway walked a few paces away in the grass and threw
up. Rhodes didn't much blame him. It was hot, and Lige
didn't smell very good. The stink was much worse now that
the door had been opened. That, along with the usual chem-
ical odor of a portable outhouse, was what Rhodes had
smelled.

"I think you three should just come along with me up to
the county car," Rhodes said. "I'll have to get on the radio
and get a little help out here."

"We didn't kill him," Kyle Foster said. His face was
green. "We didn't even know he was in there."

"That's right," Ferrin said. "We didn't know he was in
there. We were just havin' a little fun."

Rhodes looked back at the open door. "It wasn't much
fun for him, was it?"

Ferrin just looked at him.

* * *

Ruth Grady was back from Thurston by the time Rhodes got Hack on the radio, so he told Hack to have her come out and take the three prisoners into town. He also told Hack to call the ambulance and the justice of the peace.

"And see if Lawton can remember what he heard about Lige Ward," he said before he signed off.

After Ruth had loaded up the prisoners but before the ambulance arrived, Rhodes took some Polaroids of Lige and the outhouse, and then he looked the toilet over as carefully as he could. He didn't find a thing out of the ordinary, but he did dig out a couple of slugs from the walls.

The only unusual thing, if you could call it that, was the fact that Ward's clothing wasn't in the position Rhodes would have expected if Ward had been in the outhouse to use it for its intended purpose. Ward's pants were securely belted at the waist, which meant to Rhodes that Ward had probably not been shot in the silver building. Besides, the seat was down. Ward had been shot somewhere else and placed in the outhouse later.

Rhodes continued his examination. He'd have Ruth come back out and go over the portable toilet for fingerprints, but he didn't have much faith that that process would provide anything useful. He'd never been involved with a single case that was solved by fingerprints. He believed in talking to people and listening to what they said. It was a technique he had a lot more faith in than fingerprints, but that didn't mean he wouldn't collect all the evidence he could find.

Lige had been dead for quite a while. Rigor mortis had come and gone, and Lige's body was not pleasant to handle, not that Rhodes handled it much.

Lige had been struck at least twice by bullets, in the neck and head, but it would be up to the doctor to say whether the bullets had hit him before or after he was already dead.

Rhodes didn't know yet what caliber the bullets were, and he'd have to find that out, too, to see if they came from the pistol that he assumed belonged to Michael Ferrin.

The wounds didn't look as if they'd bled, which probably meant that they were inflicted after death, but that wasn't for Rhodes to decide.

There was blood on the shirt, so there might be an additional wound, one that Rhodes couldn't see. That one would have to wait for the autopsy.

After the JP arrived and pronounced Lige dead, which wasn't a difficult conclusion to reach, Rhodes watched while the body was loaded in the ambulance. Then he walked back through the field to Ferrin's pickup and went over it as carefully as he had examined the portable toilet.

Once again, he found nothing unusual. There was a box of shells for the .38, and there were two more beers in a cooler on the floorboard. There was the usual junk in the glove compartment—a map of Texas, a roll of toilet paper, an old stick of Big Red gum, an oil-stained red rag—but nothing that was incriminating.

Rhodes went back to his car for some yellow crime-scene ribbon and staked off the outhouse with it. He hoped no one would bother it, and he didn't think anyone would.

Now came the hard part. He had to go tell Rayjean Ward what had happened to her husband.

It wasn't going to be pleasant, and while Rhodes had handled similar jobs before, he thought it might be a good idea to take along some help.

"All right," Ivy said. "I'll go. But you owe me one."

"Whatever you say," Rhodes agreed. "How about dinner at the Jolly Tamale?"

Actually, Rhodes was hoping that Ivy would go for the dinner. He didn't get to eat Mexican food often.

Ivy knew what he was up to. "You're not getting off that easy."

Rhodes smiled ruefully. "I was afraid you'd say that. What then?"

Ivy considered it. "I'll think of something. Do you think I look okay?"

Rhodes looked her up and down and liked what he saw— her short graying hair, her trim figure in jeans and a plaid shirt, her half-smile as she waited for him to say something.

"You look fine to me," he said.

"I meant my clothes. Am I dressed all right? It's Sunday, after all."

"I don't think it matters," Rhodes said. "Not for what we're going to do."

They were heading out the door when the telephone rang. Rhodes answered it.

It was Hack. "Just got a call from Press Yardley," he said. "You'd better stop there after you talk to Miz Ward."

"What's the problem?" Rhodes asked.

"Somebody's stole a couple of his emus. He's mighty unhappy about it."

"I'll bet he is," Rhodes said. "All right. I'll stop by. Anything else?"

"Nope. Things're pretty quiet."

"Good. I'll come by the jail later. Did Lawton ever think of what he'd heard about Lige?"

"Not yet. But he still thinks it has somethin' to do with chickens."

"Not emus?"

"You want me to ask him?"

"Never mind," Rhodes said, and hung up.

Lige Ward had lived on what had been his father's farm. He had never done any farming, however. Hardly anyone in Blacklin County farmed anymore. That was another way that things had changed. Now people were raising emus instead of cotton.

The Wards's house was located near the small town of

Obert, a place where Rhodes had been spending a good bit of time lately. For a town with a population of less than two hundred, it was becoming something of the crime capital of Blacklin County.

What there was of the town sat on top of the highest hill in that part of the state. Beginning at the bottom of the hill, there was a wide curve in the road, but there was also a gravel road that went straight, bypassing the curve. Lige's house was about a quarter of a mile down the gravel road, a couple of hundred yards past Press Yardley's emu farm.

"I never thought I'd see the day when Blacklin County would be overrun by emus," Ivy said, looking out the car window as they drove by Yardley's place.

In back of the house there were pens surrounded by high wire fences where several of the big, ungainly birds were shifting around. One of them was drinking from a white plastic bucket that sat on the ground near the fence.

"How many people would you say have emus around here?" Ivy asked.

"Too many," Rhodes said. He wasn't fond of emus.

It actually wasn't the birds themselves that he disliked. What he didn't like was the trouble they caused. They were very expensive, with a breeding pair going for somewhere in the neighborhood of $25,000, which meant that within the last year or so emu rustling had become the fastest-growing crime in Texas, not just in Blacklin County.

And emu rustling wasn't like cattle rustling. It was easy. You didn't need a gooseneck trailer and a pickup truck to pull it. You could cram a couple of emus in the back seat of a mid-sized car, drive away with them, and sell them to anyone eager to get in on the newest craze, which seemed like just about everyone who had a little land and could afford to build some pens.

Emus weren't as easy to identify as cattle, either. They weren't branded, and they all looked pretty much alike.

"What good are emus, anyway?" Ivy wanted to know.

"I don't have any idea," Rhodes said. "You can ask Press Yardley when we stop by there."

"All right," Ivy said. "I think I will."

Rhodes drove into the Wards's yard, scattering a flock of guinea fowl. The birds were a little like smooth-feathered gray footballs with legs, bald heads, and red wattles. They raised quite a racket as they scurried out of Rhodes's way.

Pot-track! Pot-track! Pot-track! they squalled.

"Good watch-birds," Ivy said. "You think we ought to get a few?"

"No, thanks," Rhodes said. "But you're right. They are good watch-birds. As good as geese, but not as aggressive."

He stopped the car and they got out. The guineas ran behind the house, still pot-tracking. Rhodes and Ivy went to the door and Rhodes knocked.

Rayjean Ward looked the same as always when she answered Rhodes's knock, except that Rhodes thought he detected more than a hint of anxiety in her narrow eyes.

"Hello, Sheriff," she said. "Miz Rhodes. What can I do for you?"

"We're here about Lige," Rhodes said.

"Oh." Rayjean's shoulders sagged. "Did you find him?"

"You could say that," Rhodes told her. "Can we come in?"

Rayjean stood aside and held the door wide. "Sure. I didn't mean to forget my manners."

Rhodes and Ivy went inside, and Rayjean closed the door behind them. "Come on in the livin' room. I was watchin' some old Randolph Scott movie on TV."

They followed her into a small room where a 27-inch Emerson stereo TV was flickering in black and white. Rhodes caught a quick glimpse of Randolph Scott and wondered if the movies he'd taped were being run for a second time. He'd never gotten to see the ending of *Decision at Sundown.*

Rayjean noticed that Rhodes was looking at the TV. "Lige brought that TV home from the hardware store right before we closed it. He could've bought one at Wal-Mart cheaper than he could order it wholesale at the store, but he wouldn't do that. He's never set foot in that store, not past the exit door, anyhow. Why don't you two have a seat?"

Since Rayjean took her own seat in a cane-bottom rocker by the TV set, Rhodes and Ivy sat on the couch. It was covered in gray cloth, and Rhodes thought it was too soft.

"When's the last time you saw Lige?" Rhodes asked when he had sunk into the couch as far as he thought he would sink.

"It was yesterday afternoon," Rayjean said. "He had something to do, and he said he'd be back by dark. But he never came."

"You didn't call us," Rhodes said.

Rayjean didn't say anything. She just sat there, her back stiff, the rocker unmoving. Her feet were flat on the floor, and her hands rested on her knees.

Ivy spoke up. "It wasn't the first time he's stayed away, was it?"

"No," Rayjean said. "It wasn't the first time."

There was a pause. Rhodes didn't know what to say, so he didn't say anything. Ivy seemed to be waiting for Rayjean to say more, and Rhodes was content to wait as well.

Finally Rayjean said, "He drinks a little bit." She looked at Ivy. "It's only since the store closed. He never did before."

There was another pause.

"But he always came home before," Rayjean said. "Maybe he'd stay out all night now and then, but he was always home by mornin'."

"Not this morning, though," Ivy said.

Rayjean shook her head. "No, ma'am, not this mornin'. But I wasn't too worried till this afternoon. I started to get worried about dinnertime. Lige isn't one to miss his dinner.

I expect he'll be wanting supper mighty bad. Where'd you say he was?"

"We didn't say," Ivy told her. "He won't be coming home, Rayjean."

Rayjean leaned forward in the chair. "Why not? Is he in the jail?"

"No," Rhodes said. "He's dead, Mrs. Ward."

Rayjean slumped back in the chair, wrapped her arms around her thin body and started rocking. Her eyes were closed, and she was making a sound that sounded like "huhn, huhn, huhn."

Ivy stood up and went to put her arm around Rayjean. "Why don't you go get her a drink of water, Dan," she said.

Rhodes got up and went into the kitchen, which was right next to the living room. It took him two tries to find the cabinet with the glasses in it. He held the glass under the sink faucet and turned on the water. When the glass was nearly full, he went back into the living room.

Rayjean's tightly controlled hair had come partially undone; a thin tendril hung down on her right cheek. Her eyes were open, and she was no longer sobbing.

Rhodes handed her the glass of water. She took it and drank two quick sips, like a mechanical bird.

"How did it happen?" she said.

"We don't know that yet," Rhodes told her. "Are you sure you don't know where he went yesterday?"

"I told you, he didn't say."

"Did he mention the Palm Club?" Rhodes asked. That was where Lige had gotten into a little trouble in the past.

Rayjean shook her head resolutely. "No. I told you. He never said anything about where he was goin'. Why can't you tell me what happened to him?"

"He's at Ballinger's right now," Rhodes said. Clyde Ballinger was the Clearview funeral director. "You can see him later tonight."

"Is there someone we can call?" Ivy asked. "Someone who can stay with you?"

"My sister," Rayjean said. She gave them the number, and Rhodes went into the kitchen to make the call.

When he came back, Rayjean was more composed, and Rhodes thought he could get away with a few questions.

"Can you think of anyone who might have wanted to hurt Lige?" he asked. "Anyone who might have had a fight with him recently?"

"Did somebody hurt him?" Rayjean asked. "You haven't told me what happened."

Ivy looked at Rhodes. He decided he'd better open up a little.

"It looks as if someone may have shot him," he said. "But we're not sure of that. It could have been something else entirely."

"I can't believe that," Rayjean declared. "Everybody liked Lige. He was a well-respected merchant when we had the store, and people still remember that."

"What about the neighbors? Any quarrels?"

"No, never. Everyone around here liked Lige."

Rhodes thought he detected a little uncertainty in her answer.

"What about Press Yardley?" he asked.

"Press?" she said, a little too quickly, Rhodes thought. "Why, he and Lige were friends. He'd never hurt Lige."

"Didn't he get upset by your guineas?"

"Oh, there was that, but it didn't mean anything. I'd really rather not talk about it anymore, Sheriff, if that's all right with you. Maybe later I can think better."

Rhodes said that would be all right. He would talk to her again before the funeral.

"What do you think?" Ivy said when she and Rhodes were in the county car again.

"About what?"

"Did she do it?"

"What makes you think that?"

"The wife's always the first suspect in a case like that, isn't she?"

"A case like what?" Rhodes asked.

"You know. The husband is drinking too much, leaving her alone. He had to close his store, and he probably wasn't much fun to have around the house all the time."

Rhodes smiled. "I guess I shouldn't be considering retirement anytime soon."

"It wouldn't bother me," Ivy said. "Not as long as I didn't give up my job."

"At least you don't have to worry about elections," Rhodes said. "Anyway, I don't think she killed him."

"Why not?"

"I don't think she's strong enough to put him in that portable toilet."

"What if he was already in there?"

"I hadn't thought of that," Rhodes admitted.

"And what about the emus?" Ivy said. "Could that be connected?"

That was something Rhodes *had* thought about. Yardley was right next door to Lige, after all.

"We'll see," he said.

Press Yardley had called himself an antique dealer before he quit to go into the emu business, though Rhodes thought a more accurate term would have been "junk dealer." He had kept a few items from his store and he sold something now and then, things like churns, doorstops, lightning rods, and whatever else he had picked up cheap and could sell at a hefty profit.

There was a barbed-wire fence around Yardley's property, and the open gate was flanked by two remnants of the antique trade, huge wooden Indians, nearly ten feet tall. They had once been brightly painted, but the paint had mostly faded or flaked off by now, and one of the Indians had been attacked by termites. He looked as if he might have a bad case of smallpox. A hand-painted sign beside him said,

ANTIQUES FOR SALE
MONDAY–SATURDAY 9:00–5:00
CLOSED ON SUNDAY

There was another sign, too, that said, BEWARE OF THE DOG.

Rhodes pulled up beside the house and stopped. The emus didn't seem disturbed at all by the noise of the car, but a large collie dog, no doubt the one to beware of, ran out from the garage and started barking. The barking didn't bother the emus any more than the car had.

The dog ran to the car and jumped up on the door. He put his paws on the window glass and continued to bark. He looked to Rhodes to be about three-fourths collie and one-fourth something unidentifiable.

Rhodes sat in the car until Press Yardley came out of the garage and called off the dog. The animal trotted over to Yardley and tried to jump up on him and lick his face. Yardley put a knee into his stomach and took him to the garage, where he clipped the dog's collar to a chain that was attached to the garage wall.

"He wouldn't hurt you," Yardley said when Rhodes got out of the car. Yardley was a soft, round man with short arms and short legs. "He damn sure didn't hurt whoever it was that got my emus."

"Didn't he bark?" Rhodes asked.

"If he did, I didn't hear him."

"When were they stolen?"

Yardley didn't know exactly. "Probably last night. I went into Obert for a few minutes. Had to buy some groceries. It could've been then."

"You didn't leave anyone here to watch the birds?" Rhodes asked. It was a legitimate question; there were some emu owners who wouldn't even think about leaving home without posting an armed guard.

"Of course not," Yardley said. "I live off the main road, and nobody ever comes by here. I didn't think anyone even knew I had emus."

"Somebody did," Rhodes pointed out. "When did you find out the birds were missing?"

"Just this afternoon. I came out to look at them and noticed that they weren't all in the pen. I thought some of them might be in the barn there."

He pointed to a low building that didn't look much like a barn to Rhodes. It was connected to the pens and the birds could go in and out.

"But they weren't in the barn," Rhodes said.

"No, they weren't. And they aren't anywhere on the place. You've got to do something, Sheriff. Those birds were worth a lot of money."

"Were they a breeding pair?"

"No, thank goodness. They were two females. I want them back."

Rhodes looked at the gravel drive. Not much chance of tire tracks there, but the ground over by the pens was soft. If whoever had stolen the birds had driven to the fence, there might be an impression. Or maybe there were foot-prints. He walked over to look.

"Don't go over by the gate," Rhodes told Ivy, who was coming along to look at the emus. "There might be some prints there."

Ivy turned aside and walked up to the fence well away from the gate. She put her fingers in the wire and looked through the fence at the emus. Most of them were about as tall as she was, and some of them were even taller. They had grayish-brown feathers and partially bald heads that looked almost blue. One of them made a noise that sounded a little like a bass drum.

"What are they good for, anyway?" she asked Yardley, who had followed Rhodes to the fence.

"Good for? You mean you don't know?" Yardley appeared astonished to hear that there was anyone who hadn't heard all about emus.

"I really don't," Ivy said. "I thought you could tell me, if you don't mind."

"I don't mind. They're pretty interesting, actually. For one thing, you know how everyone always tells you that some kind of meat you've never tried before tastes like chicken?"

"Yes," Ivy said. "I've been told that about rattlesnake and alligator both. Are you saying that emus taste like chicken?"

"Nope. That's the best part. They're birds, but they *don't* taste like chicken. They've got red meat that's more like beef, except that it's higher in protein and lower in cholesterol and fat. And their hide's good for leather, just like a cow's. Not only that, they've got a strip of fat that runs down their backs. You can render that down and use it in cosmetics. Cures arthritis, too."

Ivy watched the big birds stalking around. They weren't much to look at, though, if Yardley was telling the truth, it was no wonder that everyone wanted to raise them.

"Are they hard to take care of?" she asked.

"Nope. They don't need much acreage to roam around in, they don't get any diseases, and the females can give you as many as forty chicks a year if you're lucky. Besides that, it costs about forty dollars a month to feed one. Try to feed a cow for that."

"But what do you do with them? I know you said the meat is good and that you can make cosmetics from the fat—"

"Don't forget about curing arthritis," Yardley said.

"—and cure arthritis, but I haven't seen any emu meat for sale in the stores. I haven't seen any advertisements for emu-based skin creams or arthritis cures. And I don't think I've ever seen any emu-skin boots."

Yardley sighed. "I know what you're thinking. You're thinking that the only people making any money from emus are the ones who sell them to people like me. But you're wrong." He thought about it. "Well, I guess you're partially right. But you just wait. In five or six years, there'll be slaughterhouses all around to take advantage of the meat and the hides. And another thing. I hear that some scientists are trying to transplant emu corneas in human eyes. And it's working! If that's right, everybody in the state will be trying to get into the business."

"It looks to me like everybody is trying to do that now," Rhodes said, joining them.

"Not everybody. It's a breeder's market right now, though, that's for sure. I was going to sell a couple of my females to Nard King, but . . ."

"What's the matter?" Rhodes asked.

"You know Nard King?"

"I don't think so."

"He lives on down this road, about half a mile past Lige Ward's place. Bought the old Garrett place about a month ago to put in an emu farm. I wonder if he decided that he could get those birds cheaper by stealing them than by paying for them. He might have, if he's got his pens finished yet."

"He's just getting started on the building?" Rhodes said.

"Yes, but it's going to be a big operation when he's done. He's getting a lot of pens built already; and he was looking around for some birds. A lot of birds. I don't think he could get as many as he wanted in one place, so he's been talking to a lot of owners. As many as he wants, the price would add up."

"Could you identify your emus if I found them?"

"I think so," Yardley said, but he didn't look too sure of it.

"I guess I'd better talk to King, then," Rhodes said.

Yardley agreed. "I think that would be a good idea."

"I'll do it. There's something else I want to do, too. I'll be sending a deputy out to make some casts of impressions around this fence. Don't go walking around out here until that's done."

"You found something?" Yardley said.

Rhodes was noncommittal. "Maybe. I'll let you know. Meanwhile, you need to keep a better watch on these pens."

"Maybe I should just buy a better dog."

"Or you could get some guineas," Ivy said.

It was a hot day, and Yardley's round face was already red, but now it got redder still. "Don't talk to me about guineas. I've had to listen to those stupid birds of Lige Ward's cackling day and night for years."

In fact, Rhodes remembered, it was the noise from the guineas that had prompted Yardley's calls to the sheriff's department to complain about his neighbor.

"If it was up to me," Yardley continued, "there wouldn't be any guineas left in the world."

"They might scare away a bird rustler," Rhodes said.

"I'd rather have rustlers, then. Don't talk to me about any guineas."

Rhodes and Ivy got into the county car and drove through Yardley's gate. As they passed the wooden Indians, Ivy started humming "Kaw-Liga."

"You're dating yourself," Rhodes told her.

"I was thinking about the Charlie Pride version," Ivy said. "Not the one by Hank Williams."

"Oh."

"So who's showing his age now?"

"Me, I guess," Rhodes said.

Ivy changed the subject. "Do you think he did it?"

"Did what? Stole his own emus?"

"I hadn't thought of that," Ivy said. "I meant, do you think he killed Lige Ward?"

"You mean you don't think Lige's wife did it?"

Ivy made a fist and hit Rhodes in the shoulder. "Maybe she did. But Mr. Yardley got really upset when I mentioned those guineas."

Rhodes had to admit that she was right. "But I don't think he'd kill somebody just because those birds were too noisy."

"You never know about some people," Ivy said.

Rhodes nodded. She was right about that, too.

4

▼

RHODES DIDN'T GO DIRECTLY TO KING'S PLACE. THAT WOULD have to wait. Instead he took Ivy home, told her that he probably wouldn't be back in time for supper, and drove to Clyde Ballinger's funeral home, a huge red brick building that had once been Clearview's most impressive mansion. The green lawn was shaded by tall oak trees, and there was a metal statue of a mountain lion or some such animal in the front yard.

Ballinger had his private office in the small house behind the main building. He regarded the office as his special place, and he didn't allow many visitors to enter it. Rhodes was one of those who had the privilege.

Rhodes knocked on the door and went in without waiting for an answer. He knew that Ballinger would be on the premises, what with a "client" having been sent by the sheriff's department.

He was right. Ballinger was sitting at his old wooden desk, his feet propped up on top of it, reading a book. A lover of old paperback mystery and crime novels that he bought at garage sales, he was always reading when he got the chance.

He put his feet down when he saw Rhodes and stuck a

piece of paper in the book he had been reading before closing it.

"Hey, Sheriff," he said. "You're causing more trouble, I see."

"I'm not the one causing it," Rhodes said. "I'm just trying to keep up with it."

"You're causing it for *me*," Ballinger pointed out. "That's what I meant. And now I'm about to cause it for you."

"How?" Rhodes asked.

"You can't get an autopsy done here anymore, that's how."

Ballinger was short and fat, and he was usually smiling and happy, the exact opposite of everyone's idea of a funeral director. But today he wasn't smiling. He didn't look at all happy, either.

"Why not?" Rhodes asked. "What's the matter?"

"Dr. White says he's not going to do it anymore. He says that it's too dangerous."

"Dangerous?" Rhodes said. He knew that some people in Ballinger's business were fearful of contracting blood-transmitted diseases. Maybe White was, too. "Is he afraid of getting AIDS?"

"It's not that," Ballinger said. "He's afraid of going to jail."

"Jail? Why would he be worried about that?"

"Don't you keep up with things?" Ballinger asked. "Didn't you read about that doctor out in west Texas that got into all that trouble?"

"Oh," Rhodes said.

He'd read some of the stories, all right. He didn't remember the exact situations, but he thought that the doctor had been a county medical examiner or something along that line; he'd also been very careless in some of his decisions and with some of the bodies he'd worked on. There had been numerous lawsuits and exhumations, and some judge was making noises about freeing every prisoner convicted on evidence obtained from the doctor's autopsies. Rhodes thought he even remembered something about a head getting lost.

"I'll talk to Dr. White," Rhodes said. "This has to be done fast."

"Won't work," Ballinger said. "He won't do it."

"He'll do it," Rhodes said. "I'll make him an offer he can't refuse."

Ballinger didn't ask what that might be, and the thought of it didn't seem to cheer him up any.

"Is there something else?" Rhodes asked him.

"Yeah," Ballinger said. "There is."

He picked up the book and held it so that Rhodes could see the title. It was *The Mugger*.

"You see the author's name?" Ballinger asked.

Rhodes saw the name, but he had to look for a second to find it. It was in yellow letters in the lower left-corner of the cover. It was the name of one of Ballinger's favorite writers.

"Ed McBain," Rhodes said.

"That's right. And that's what's bothering me."

"The name?" There were times when Rhodes wasn't sure that he knew exactly what was going on, and this was one of them.

"Not the name," Ballinger said. "You know it's not his real name, don't you?"

Rhodes was getting more and more lost. "Whose real name?"

"Ed McBain's. His real name is Evan Hunter, except that's not it, either."

"It's not?"

"No, and Richard Marsten's not his real name, either."

Rhodes just sat there, wondering how they'd gotten onto this subject in the first place.

"I don't know what his real name is," Ballinger said. "It doesn't matter, anyhow. Those other names are just pen names that he uses. Like Ed McBain." Ballinger dropped the book to the desk. "Can you copyright a name?"

Rhodes didn't know.

"Well, you should be able to. He used Ed McBain first, and now everybody else is using it. He ought to be able to sue."

Rhodes thought he was beginning to catch on. "Someone else is using the name Ed McBain?"

"Not the Ed part. Just the McBain. It was 'The Simpsons' that did it first."

"Who're the Simpsons?"

"It's not a who. It's a what, a cartoon TV show; it's pretty funny, most of the time. Anyway, they did this parody of Arnold Schwarzenegger movies and called it *McBain.* I thought that was okay, but the other day I saw this new movie on videotape. It was called *McBain,* so I rented it. Pitiful, just pitiful. Christopher Walken. You know who he is?"

Rhodes was on safe ground now. He knew movie actors. "He was in *The Deer Hunter.*"

"Yeah, if you say so. And now he's McBain. I'll tell you, the real McBain should be able to sue."

"We're talking about *Ed* McBain now?"

"That's right," Ballinger said. "Or whatever his real name is. He should be able to sue. All those other people are capitalizing on his name."

"I'd like to help him out, but it's not in my jurisdiction," Rhodes said, hoping to bring the conversation to an end. "Can I use your telephone? I need to call Dr. White."

Rhodes was able to persuade White that no one was going to sue him, and he didn't mention Ballinger's idea for a lawsuit against the people who were using the name McBain.

He didn't make the doctor any special offers; instead he told him what a great job he'd always done for the county and how much he was appreciated. He mentioned the fact that if White didn't do the job, the body would have to be sent to a forensics lab and days would elapse before Rhodes got any results. After a few minutes of that sort of thing, White agreed to come into town and perform the autopsy.

After the phone call, Rhodes asked Ballinger about Lige Ward's personal property.

"There's not much," Ballinger said. "Just the clothes, and I didn't go through them. You want to do that?"

Rhodes said that he did. Ruth would already have vacuumed the clothing for hair and fibers, which Rhodes didn't think would be admitted as evidence, considering where the body had been found, but there might be something in the pockets.

Rhodes and Ballinger walked over to the main building. On a table in a small white-walled room in the rear lay Lige Ward's clothing—overalls, shirt, shoes, underwear, Astros cap. It wasn't much, as Ballinger had said.

Rhodes took his reading glasses out of his shirt pocket, put them on, and started going through the clothes. The heels of the shoes were filthy and scuffed, and there was dirt on the back of the pants and shirt. Rhodes thought that Ward had been shot and then dragged to the portable outhouse. He'd have to remember to ask the doctor about that later. He scraped some of the dirt into an evidence bag before going through the rest of the clothes.

There was nothing in the shirt pocket, nothing in the hat or shoes. There was a billfold in the back pocket of the jeans. It contained twenty-three dollars, a driver's license, a social security card, and a Visa card.

In the deep side pockets of the overalls, Rhodes found sixty-eight cents in change, an Old Timer pocket knife, and some car keys. Where was Ward's pickup? he wondered. That was something that had to be looked into.

There was one other thing in the pockets. It was a metal spike about two inches long with a hook at one end.

Rhodes held it up and looked at it.

"A gaff," Ballinger said. "Like they use on fighting roosters. There's an old paperback book about rooster fighting. It's called *Cockfighter,* by a guy named Charles Willeford. He wrote a lot of stuff for the paperbacks. I've got one called *High Priest of California,* and I think—"

"Never mind that," Rhodes said. He didn't want to get into another discussion of paperback writers. "The question is, how did this gaff get in Lige's pocket?"

Ballinger studied the wicked-looking piece of steel. "I'd say, just guessing now, that he put it there."

"I know he put it there. Or somebody did. But I wonder why. It's not the kind of thing a man just carries around."

Then Rhodes remembered what Lawton had said about Lige Ward. Chickens. Maybe he hadn't meant chickens. Maybe he'd meant roosters. Or fighting cocks.

"There's not any cockfighting around here, is there?" Ballinger asked.

"There shouldn't be," Rhodes told him. "It's illegal."

Ballinger nodded, then said, "From what I hear, that doesn't bother some people."

Rhodes took off his reading glasses and put them back in his shirt pocket. "What people?"

"Nobody in particular," Ballinger said. "But there's been cockfighting in Texas just about forever, whether it's legal or not. I guess you know there's people right here in Blacklin County that raise fighting cocks."

"There's nothing illegal about raising them," Rhodes said. "Just fighting them."

Ballinger stared reflectively at the ceiling of the white room. "I read about a case down around Houston not long ago. The Texas Rangers raided a big cockfight, arrested nearly a hundred people. One of 'em was interviewed by the paper. Said getting arrested didn't bother him, that he'd just pay his fine and go home and that there'd be another fight somewhere the next weekend."

"He was probably right," Rhodes admitted. "It's hard to control. The cockfighters even publish a magazine, but they don't advertise the fights in it, not the ones in Texas."

"What about other states? It's legal in some places, isn't it? How about Mexico?"

"It's not legal in Mexico," Rhodes said. "But there's a lot of it that goes on there, and in Texas too, down on the border. It's legal in *New* Mexico, though. They've written their cruelty-to-animals statutes to be sure cockfighting's specifically excluded."

"But it's not legal in Texas."

"Not in Texas," Rhodes agreed. "There's not supposed to be any of that here."

"Except that thing you're holding in your hand's a gaff for a fighting cock."

"Right. Except for that."

Rhodes was looking down at the floor now. "What's that?" he asked, pointing.

The floor was as white and clean as the rest of the room, but there was something reddish brown lying near Ballinger's right foot.

"It must've come from Lige's clothes," Ballinger said. "Whatever it is."

Rhodes bent down and started to pick it up. It drifted away from him and he had to reach again. That time he got it.

"It's a feather," he said, straightening up.

"What kind of feather?" Ballinger asked.

Rhodes couldn't answer that, but he would have bet on one of two things: it came from either an emu or a fighting cock.

It was about five o'clock when Rhodes arrived at the jail. There was still plenty of daylight left, and he would go back to Obert to talk to Nard King later. Right now, he wanted to talk to Lawton.

The jailer wasn't in the office when Rhodes entered. Hack was there, however, and so was his friend, Mrs. McGee. In spite of the heat, she was, as usual, wearing a sweater and a knitted cap that was pulled down over her ears.

"How are you, Mrs. McGee?" Rhodes asked.

"I'm just fine, thank you, Sheriff," she said.

She and Hack were watching a small television set that was sitting in the middle of Hack's desk.

"What's that?" Rhodes asked, indicating the set.

"Mega Watchman," Hack said. "Miz McGee brought it over here so I could watch TV. Pretty good picture, don't you think?"

The picture was so small that Rhodes could hardly see it from across the room. He walked over closer to the desk.

"'Course we can't get anything but the close-by stations," Hack said. "None of that cable stuff. But that's better than nothin'."

While Hack hadn't been wanting a television set for as long as he'd been wanting a computer, he'd said more than once that it would be nice to have one at the station. The set was tuned in to a Texas Rangers game.

"The prisoners are going to complain more than ever now," Rhodes said. There was no television in the cells.

"Too bad," Hack said. He plainly didn't care. He was just interested in watching the game.

Rhodes supposed there was nothing wrong with having a TV set in the office, as long as it didn't interfere with the work. He didn't watch much himself, unless there was an old movie on.

"Better take a break," he told Hack. "I want you to put out an APB on Lige Ward's pickup. I didn't see it at his house. You can use that computer of yours to find out the make and model and license number."

Hack liked nothing better than a chance to use the computer. "I've already checked the serial number of that pistol you tagged and bagged. It's supposed to belong to some fella in Wichita Falls, but you can bet he sold it to somebody who sold it to somebody else who sold it to somebody else."

"Give him a call anyway," Rhodes said.

"Sure thing. But right now I got to look up that pickup truck." Hack turned from the game and started tapping away.

"Where's Lawton?" Rhodes asked before Hack got too involved.

Hack looked up from the monitor. "He's up in the cell-block with those three fellas Ruth brought in. They're gripin' because it's takin' the bondsman too long to get here."

"I'd better talk to them before he does," Rhodes said. Lawton could wait; not that Rhodes expected to get much out of the three men.

And he didn't. All three denied ownership of the pistol, and Rhodes was sure there wouldn't be any help from the man in Wichita Falls. The pistol could easily have been bought at a flea market somewhere. Ferrin claimed that they had found it.

"What about the cartridges?" Rhodes asked him. "Did you find those, too?"

"Bought 'em at Wal-Mart," Ferrin said.

It seemed easy enough for him to remember that, but the other two remembered it as well. It had been a big production for them to decide which one was sober enough to go into the store and make the purchase.

"Where did you find the pistol?" Rhodes asked.

Ferrin couldn't remember, nor could the other two, or so they said. Rhodes thought that they might even be telling the truth, since they hadn't had any time together to get their stories straight, unless they'd managed to do it in the back of the car when Ruth was bringing them in. Rhodes didn't think that was the case.

There was one thing on which Kyle Foster and Larry Galloway agreed, however, and that was who found the pistol. Both of them were sure it was Ferrin.

"I know because he was the one doin' most of the shootin'," Foster said. "If I'd've found it, I'd be the one who got to shoot it."

Rhodes questioned each of the three men separately in different cells, and the story that he pieced together was that they'd started drinking on Saturday night at the Palm Club and had continued on well into Sunday morning. They'd gone to Ferrin's house after the Palm Club closed down.

Ferrin left the other two there and went out to buy beer. He'd come back with a lot of it, a case or two or three, and they'd drunk some more. Then they slept for a couple of hours. When they woke up, they started drinking again.

After a while, they decided that it was a pretty day and that they should get out and enjoy the sunshine. They'd driven around in Ferrin's pickup, still drinking, for an unspecified length of time—none of them could remember how long—before they ran across the portable toilet and decided to have some fun with it. Somewhere in there, Ferrin, or someone, had found the pistol, but everyone was vague about that part.

Now that the three of them hadn't had a drink for a good while, none of them was feeling so well. Their complexions were grayish green, and their eyes were red. Rhodes could tell that they would've liked to go somewhere nicer than a jail cell and lie down for a long time.

But he kept after them, questioning them about the portable toilet and the pistol. "Did you find them together or in different places?" he asked Ferrin.

Ferrin's hat was on the iron cot in the cell, and he put his hands up to the sides of his head. "I can't remember. I told you ten times I couldn't remember. Why don't you just leave me alone?"

"Because there was a dead man in that toilet, and you were shooting at it. Maybe you even killed him. That's why."

"I didn't kill anybody!" Ferrin said. "We just found the damn pistol and we thought it'd be fun to shoot at somethin'. That's all there was to it."

"Maybe," Rhodes said. "But maybe not. I'll be talking to you again."

Ferrin didn't say anything; he just sat with his head between his hands, as if trying to hold it together.

"If I were you, I'd try to remember where I found that pistol," Rhodes said before he left the cell.

Ferrin just grunted. Rhodes couldn't tell if that was a yes or a no.

All three of them probably knew that Rhodes didn't really have anything on them other than a few misdemeanor charges: public intoxication, creating a disturbance, and unlawful possession of a firearm. The last one was a Class A, but it still wasn't a felony. He'd keep hammering at them anyway.

Lawton was waiting in the office when Rhodes came back down. He was over by Hack's desk watching the Ranger game.

"Cockfighting," Rhodes said.

Lawton's head jerked up. "That's it! That's what I heard about Lige Ward. How'd you know, Sheriff?"

Rhodes resisted the urge to say that a little bird had told him. He reached into his pocket and brought out the gaff.

"Ever see one of these before?"

Miz McGee and Hack looked too. Miz McGee didn't appear to know what it was, but Hack did. So did Lawton.

"It's a gaff like they use on fightin' cocks," Lawton said. "But it don't look quite right, someway."

"What way?" Rhodes asked.

"Hand it here," Hack said, and Rhodes gave it to him.

Hack looked at the gaff, then handed it to Lawton. "I see it. How 'bout you?"

Lawton examined the piece of steel, then ran his finger along it. "Sure. Somebody's filed an edge on the bottom. Usually a gaff is just round, like a needle, but this one's more like a sword."

He handed the gaff back to Rhodes, who took it and ran his thumb along the sharpened edge. It was not quite as keen as a razor blade, but it would do.

"Yeah, it's like a sword," Hack said. "See, a round one, which is the way they usually are, will generally just slide off if it hits a bone. But one with an edge on it like that, it's likely to penetrate. Maybe break the bone."

"That's not fair, is it?" Mrs. McGee said.

"Who cares?" Hack said. "Cockfightin's illegal anyway, so what's one more crooked trick? What're you gonna do if you catch somebody at it? Go to the sheriff?" He looked at Rhodes. "Where'd you get that thing, anyhow?"

"Lige had it," Rhodes said. "It was in his pocket."

"Not the kinda thing a fella'd usually be carryin' around," Lawton said. "Unless he had somethin' to do with cockfightin'."

"Did he?" Rhodes asked. "You said you'd heard something. And you and Hack seem to know an awful lot about cockfighting."

"I heard somethin', all right," Lawton admitted. "But you know how that is. You can't put any faith in what you hear."

"Tell me anyway," Rhodes said.

"Well," Lawton began, "this was before your time, I guess, but Lige Ward's daddy—"

"What does Lige's daddy have to do with this?" Rhodes asked, trying to keep Lawton on the subject. If he let the jailer get started down a sidetrack, they might never get to the point. Hack and Lawton were worse than Ballinger when it came to meandering all over the place.

9 4 - 1 5 3 1 7

"I was tryin' to tell you what he has to do with it," Lawton said. "If you'll just let me get to it."

Rhodes walked over and sat down at his desk. He might as well make himself comfortable.

"Sorry. I didn't mean to interrupt. You go on ahead."

"You do that a lot lately," Hack said. "Interrupt, I mean."

Rhodes took a deep breath. "I said I was sorry. Go on, Lawton. What about Lige's father?"

"His name was Smokey," Lawton said. "'Course that wasn't his real name. People just called him that."

A strong feeling of déjà vu came over Rhodes, but he kept his mouth shut. He knew it wouldn't do any good to ask what Ward's real name had been. He just hoped it didn't turn out to be Ed McBain.

It didn't.

"His real name was Elton," Lawton said. "I don't know why they called him Smokey. But anyway, back in the thirties, Smokey raised fightin' roosters out there on that place of his close to Obert."

That was news to Rhodes, but as Lawton had said, it was before Rhodes's time.

"Had him some pretty good birds," Hack said. "Fought 'em, too." He glanced at Mrs. McGee, who was looking at him with disapproval. "Not that I ever went to any of the fights myself, mind you. I just heard about 'em."

"Yeah," Lawton said. "Me, too. Anyway, he quit durin' the war. I don't know why. Maybe there was too many men off fightin' in the war for there to be any crowds for a cockfight. But I guess Lige must've known about those roosters. Maybe he even remembered 'em."

Rhodes thought they were getting somewhere now. "Did he ever raise them himself?"

Lawton shook his head. "Not that I ever heard of."

"Then what was the connection between Lige and cock-fighting?"

OZARKS REGIONAL LIBRARY
217 EAST DICKSON ST.
FAYETTEVILLE, ARKANSAS 72701

Lawton gave Rhodes a hurt look. "I was gettin' to that part."

Rhodes forced himself to relax. "Sorry. I didn't mean to rush you."

"You been doin' a lot of *that* lately, too," Hack said. "Rushin' people. I'm beginnin' to wonder if gettin' married was good for you."

"That's the truth," Lawton said. "Bein' married don't agree with just ever'body. I remember—"

"Lige Ward," Rhodes said. He couldn't help himself. "Cockfighting."

"Cranky," Hack said. "You're gettin' downright cranky."

Rhodes didn't apologize this time. He just waited for Lawton to get on with his story, which he finally did.

"Well, anyway, I was out at Wal-Mart, sittin' on the bench in the entranceway there, when Gad Pullens came in. He sat down, and we got started talkin' about first one thing and then another, and I said somethin' about how Lige Ward sure did hate Wal-Mart, and Gad mentioned something about how it was a shame that Lige had closed up his store and how he'd heard that Lige was thinkin' about maybe stagin' a cockfight to make a little money."

"You heard that there was going to be a cockfight, and you didn't think about mentioning it to me?" Rhodes said.

"Downright cranky," Hack said under his breath, though not so low that Rhodes couldn't hear him.

"I didn't hear that there was gonna *be* a cockfight," Lawton said. "Or I'd've told you. I heard that Lige was *thinkin'* about havin' one. That's all. I didn't really believe it, and I guess that's why I forgot about it. He couldn't make much money that way, nohow."

"Depends on how much the entrants had to put up," Hack said. "And on how much prize money he gave out."

"Just when was this fight supposed to be?" Rhodes asked Lawton.

"I told you I didn't know that there *was* goin' to be one. That was a good while back. If there was a fight, it's all over by now."

"Maybe there's been more than one," Hack said. "I'll ask around if you think it might help."

"Me, too," Lawton said.

"Talk to Gad Pullens," Rhodes told Lawton. "See if you can find out who's raising fighting cocks, aside from the two or three we already know about. And get me another one of these gaffs if you can. File it till it's just like this one." He turned to Hack. "Did you get out that APB on Lige's pickup?"

"Sure did. It's a black Ford Ranger." He gave Rhodes the license number, and Rhodes wrote it down. "Anything else you want?"

"Yes," Rhodes said. "Have Ruth go out to Press Yardley's and take some impressions of the footprints around his emu pens. The ones close to the gate. While she's out there, get her to take one of Press's shoes, so we can eliminate them."

Rhodes didn't have much more faith in footprints than he did in fingerprints, but you could never tell when something would turn out to be useful.

"And first thing tomorrow," he continued, "call up the people who rent out those Sani-Cans. Tell them there's one missing, and try to find out where it was."

Hack didn't write anything down. He prided himself on being able to remember. "Is that all?"

"You can run a man named Nard King through that computer of yours. His whole first name's probably Bernard."

Hack nodded. "That it?"

"For now. If you hear from Dr. White about the autopsy, call me at home."

"Even if it's late?" Hack said.

"That's right," Rhodes told him. "Even if it's late."

5

▼

BEFORE GOING BACK OUT TO OBERT TO TALK TO NARD KING, Rhodes drove by the veterinary clinic owned by Dr. Slick, who had recently helped Rhodes with a case involving cattle rustling. Slick's house was located only a few yards away from the clinic, and Rhodes was hoping that the vet would be home on a late Sunday afternoon.

Rhodes was in luck. Slick came to the door and asked Rhodes in. "What brings you by here on a Sunday? Got another case I can help you with?"

"Maybe," Rhodes said. He fished the feather out of his pocket and handed it to Slick in its plastic bag. "Can you tell me what that is?"

Slick took it and looked at it closely. After a few seconds he said, "Looks like a feather to me."

Rhodes was surrounded by comedians. "I figured that out for myself. I was hoping you could tell me what *kind* of feather it is."

"It's not a chicken feather," Slick said. "I can tell you that much. I've seen plenty of chicken feathers, and this isn't one."

Rhodes waited.

"I'd guess it's an emu feather," Slick went on. "Until a

year or so ago, I'd never seen one of those, and I still don't see too many. Had an emu in the clinic the other day, though. Dog got after it. Anyway, this looks like an emu feather to me. I could examine it more carefully if it's important."

Rhodes was willing to bet that Slick was right, but he said, "If you wouldn't mind. I'd better make absolutely sure."

"I'll give your office a call tomorrow," Slick said.

Rhodes thanked him and left. For the time being, he'd work on the assumption that an emu feather had been among Lige Ward's effects. It seemed likely enough, even though the feather had been on the floor when Rhodes found it.

Rhodes drove out to Obert again as the sun began to sink behind a bank of dark clouds that lined the horizon, outlining the clouds with orange and turning the western half of the sky an orangy pink.

Rhodes wasn't in any mood to enjoy the sunset, however. He was thinking about Lige Ward. Ward had caused Rhodes a little trouble now and then, but not until he'd been forced to close his hardware store. He'd been a decent man, and now he was dead. Murdered, most likely. Someone had killed him, and Rhodes was going to find out who and why. He was confident of that, though things had already gotten very complicated.

For one thing, there were three drunks who might or might not be implicated in Lige's death, but who were surely involved with stealing the outhouse that he'd been found in.

For another thing, somebody had stolen two of Press Yardley's emus.

And it seemed at least likely that there was cockfighting going on in Blacklin County.

Besides that, there was Nard King to deal with. Though

Rhodes had no idea yet how he fit into the picture, he was sure there was bound to be a connection. Yardley had already mentioned one possibility.

Add to all that the idea that Ivy had, at least half in seriousness, suggested—that Rayjean Ward had killed her own husband.

About the only thing that hadn't been suggested, in fact, was that Hal Keene, the Wal-Mart manager, had killed Lige, and someone would surely think of that possibility before too long. It wouldn't have surprised Rhodes to hear that someone had already thought of it.

Rhodes hoped that he could get everything sorted out before something else happened, but that wasn't the way things usually worked out. Things usually got uglier than anyone would expect them to get where murder was concerned, but maybe this time could be an exception.

Rhodes hoped that would be the case, but he didn't really believe that it would.

Nard King didn't have an impressive house. It was just a little frame building that needed paint, but there would soon be a much bigger one nearby. The foundation was already poured, and the frame was up.

The pens he was building for his emus were also going to be well made, certainly the equal of any that Rhodes had seen. They were roofed with tin to provide shade, and a sizable barn had been started behind them.

There were no members of the construction crews present late on a Sunday afternoon, and there were only a few emus in the pens. Rhodes counted four. He wondered if someone living so close to Press Yardley would actually have stolen two of Yardley's birds. It would have taken a lot of nerve, that much was sure, but unless the birds were marked in some way that Rhodes didn't know about, he didn't see how Yardley could prove that they were his.

Rhodes parked in the front yard, got out of his car and stood looking around. Just forty-five or fifty yards behind King's house a thick stand of woods began, the same woods that ran behind the houses of Lige Ward and Press Yardley. It was already dark back in the trees.

There was a light breeze from the west, and Rhodes waited by the car for a minute to enjoy it. It was very quiet in the country. Rhodes thought he heard a car whoosh by on the main road, but that might have been his imagination; he was a good three-quarters of a mile from the pavement. There was also a mechanical clanking that Rhodes couldn't quite identify.

He could hear some birds down in the woods as they settled into the trees for the night, and somewhere in the distance a dog barked. Probably at Press Yardley's house.

There was a light in the front room of King's house, and Rhodes stepped up on the porch. The door opened before he could knock and a man peered at him through the screen.

"What do you want?" he said.

Rhodes identified himself and explained that he was there to ask about some stolen emus.

"Well, come on in then," King said. "If you're the sheriff, there's no use in you having to stand out there on the porch. Nobody's stolen any of my emus, though."

He pushed open the screen and Rhodes walked into the living room. The floor was bare except for a couple of throw rugs. A window-unit air conditioner clanked and clattered. That was the noise Rhodes had heard in the yard but had been unable to identify. It was much louder in the house.

There was no couch in the room, only a card table and four folding chairs. There wasn't even a TV set. A paperback book called *Sons of Liberty* was splayed spine-up on the table. A pair of half-glasses lay by the book.

King noticed Rhodes looking around the room. "I don't

have much furniture yet," he said. "I just bought this place, and I didn't want to buy anything right off. I'm waiting until I get the new house finished."

King looked to Rhodes about fifty-five. He was thin, with a tanned, wrinkled face, and he looked as if he'd spent a lot of time outdoors. He was wearing jeans and a plain cotton short-sleeved shirt. His hands were callused, and his arms were corded with muscle.

"When did you move to Obert?" Rhodes asked.

King walked over to the card table and pulled out a chair. "Have a seat. No use to stand up."

Rhodes went over and sat. King sat on the other side of the table and pushed the book out of his way.

"I've been here about a month," King said. "I moved down from Dallas. Worked at Super-Tex Freight Lines there for thirty years, mostly doing local deliveries. I retired a couple of months ago and decided to invest in an emu ranch."

"Why emus?" Rhodes asked. He was genuinely curious.

King leaned forward on the table. "Well, that's kind of interesting. I was thinking about cattle, to tell the truth. I grew up around cattle, and I always thought I'd like to have me a little ranch when I retired. So I went down to that big livestock show they have in Houston every year to see about getting started in the cattle business. While I was there, I saw this ostrich booth."

"Ostriches?"

"Right. There's a lot of ostrich ranches in Texas, but I thought better of that. They're too much trouble. They're bigger than emus, and they can hurt you if you're not careful. Kick the devil out of you, kick harder than emus, even. And they're not as resistant to disease."

"So you went with emus."

"Right. There was a booth there about them, too. I'm just getting started, but I'll have me a pretty good ranch here before long, soon as I can get me some more birds."

King looked at Rhodes sharply. "What's this about some birds being stolen, anyway? Happen around here?"

Rhodes told him about Yardley's emus.

King was thoughtful. "Yardley, huh? I talked to him about buying some of his stock, but he didn't much want to sell."

"How well do you know your other neighbors?" Rhodes asked.

"The Wards? Just well enough to talk to. I haven't seen much of 'em but they seem like nice folks. Mr. Ward doesn't like being retired as much as I do."

Rhodes told King about Lige's death. King reacted with surprise.

"Dead? Why, I just saw him—" King broke off.

"When did you see him?"

King looked at the Revolutionary soldier portrayed on the spine of *Sons of Liberty* as if the man were incredibly interesting.

Then he looked back at Rhodes. "Well, I don't remember, exactly, but it must've been just the other day."

"He was killed last night," Rhodes said. "You didn't see him then, by any chance?"

"Nope. Sure didn't. I was here reading this book last night." King reached over and pulled the book across the table. "I didn't see anybody all night. How'd he get killed? Car wreck?"

"I'm not sure," Rhodes said. He didn't see any reason yet to tell King that he was sure Ward had been murdered.

"Well, I'm sorry to hear it. Like I said, he and his wife seem like nice folks."

Rhodes brought the subject back to the emus. "What about those four emus of yours that I saw in the pens out there? Where did you buy them?"

It was cool in the room, but King was sweating. "Different places. It's hard to find any for sale around here."

"You have the bills of sale?" Rhodes asked.

"That's right. I have the bills of sale. Sure do."

"Where are they?"

King looked around the room, then looked back at the book. He reached out and turned the book around. He looked at it a second before turning it back.

"They're around here somewhere. I probably stuck 'em in a drawer."

"Why don't you see if you can find them?" Rhodes suggested.

"It might take a while," King said. "I don't really try to keep up with stuff like that. I'm not real businesslike. I just stick things someplace. Probably in a drawer."

It was Rhodes's turn to look around the room.

"There don't seem to be a lot of drawers to stick things in," he observed.

"You should see the kitchen," King said. "Cabinets and drawers all over the place. And the bedroom. It's a real mess. I have a dresser in there, and a desk, too."

"I'd still like to see those bills of sale," Rhodes said. "Even if it is a little trouble to find them."

King stood up. "Right. Well, if you'll come back tomorrow, I'll have 'em for you. It's just that I can't put my hand on 'em right this minute."

Rhodes stood up as well. "All right. I'll be back tomorrow."

"Right. I'll have those bills of sale for you, too."

"I'm sure you will," Rhodes told him.

After he left King's place, Rhodes drove back to the main road and on up the hill into Obert, past the old college and down a gravel road to the Appleby house. It was fully dark now, and Rhodes's headlights burned a tunnel down the road.

The Applebys had been involved in the cattle-rustling case that Dr. Slick had helped Rhodes with, not to mention a murder at the old college building on the hill. They were

what Rhodes supposed the newspapers would call a "dys-
functional family," but they were getting along better now
that Mr. Appleby was residing in one of the state peniten-
tiary units.

Mrs. Appleby hadn't found a job yet, but Twyla Faye,
the daughter, was working as a checker at the supermarket
next to Wal-Mart, and Claude and Clyde, the twins, were
planning to get back into school in the fall.

The Applebys were at home, as Rhodes had thought they
would be. Mrs. Appleby was glad to see the sheriff, and she
tried to get him to eat some supper.

"We just finished," she said. "There's some fried chicken
left, and some cream gravy."

Rhodes hadn't had any fried chicken or cream gravy in
months. Probably years. And now that he'd married Ivy, he
wasn't likely to have any. She was a big believer in eating
healthy foods, which was why he had tried to get her to
settle for a dinner at the Jolly Tamale.

Rhodes was strongly tempted by the offer of the fried
chicken. But he'd noticed lately that it was slightly easier to
get his belt buckled in the mornings, so he thought that he
might actually have lost a pound or two. With regret, he
declined the offer.

"Well, then, is this a social visit, or did you have some
news for us?"

"No news," Rhodes told her. "I just needed a little information, and I hoped the twins might be able to help me
out."

"They will if they can," Mrs. Appleby said. "Claude!
Clyde! You two come in here."

Rhodes knew that Mrs. Appleby would see to it that the
twins cooperated. They owed him a favor; he'd managed to
keep them out of jail by minimizing their part in the recent
Obert crime spree.

The twins came in from another room. They were big,
moon-faced young men, and Rhodes couldn't always tell

them apart. But that was all right. For what he wanted, he didn't have to know which one he was talking to.

"Sheriff Rhodes wants to say somethin' to you," Mrs. Appleby told her sons. "He says he needs a little help, and I told him you'd be glad to give it to him."

Claude and Clyde stood there looking at Rhodes. They might have appreciated what he'd done for them, but you'd never know it by looking at them.

"I'd like to talk to them alone," he told Mrs. Appleby.

"Why, sure, I understand. I'll just go in the other room and watch TV with Twyla Faye. You call me if you need anything."

"I will," Rhodes said.

When she'd gone into the other room, he turned his attention to the twins, who were still looking at him. Now that their mother was out of the room, a certain amount of wariness had entered their gaze.

"There's nothing for you to be worried about," Rhodes told them. "This isn't about you."

The twins looked at one another and then back at Rhodes. They didn't look any less apprehensive.

"It's about somebody else entirely," Rhodes assured them. "All I want to know is whether you've heard about something that might be going on around here. There's nothing wrong with hearing things."

"What things?" the twin on Rhodes's left asked. Rhodes thought that one was Claude, but he wasn't quite sure.

"I wondered if you knew anything about a cockfight," Rhodes said. "I heard there might have been one around here lately."

If there was anyone in Obert who would know about a cockfight, it was Claude and Clyde. They had a way of getting around the town and finding out things.

They didn't look as if they wanted to tell Rhodes anything, however.

"Cockfighting's against the law," the twin who might have been Claude said.

"That's right. It's against the law," the other twin—Clyde?—said piously. "And we don't have anything to do with stuff that's against the law. We've learned our lesson."

"I didn't say you had anything to do with it," Rhodes told them. "I just wondered if you might have heard something. There's no law against hearing something."

The twins looked at one another again. Rhodes wondered if there was anything to that old tale about twins' being able to communicate with one another without talking.

"Maybe we heard something," Clyde said. "But that's all. We just heard something."

Rhodes nodded to show that he understood. "Why don't you just tell me what you heard, then."

"We heard there was a cockfight out in the woods behind Lige Ward's place last month," Clyde said. "We heard that there was another one yesterday."

"Did you hear the names of anybody that was at these fights?"

"No," Claude said. "No names. Just that there was gonna be fights."

It was possible that the twins hadn't been at either fight. They might have been afraid of what would happen to them if there had been a raid. Even if they had been there, or if they had heard any names, Rhodes didn't really expect them to tell him. It didn't matter. Later, he might have to talk to them again about that, but for now he'd found out what he'd come to learn.

He thanked the twins, and they went back into the other room. Mrs. Appleby came out.

"Did they help you any?" she asked.

"They did," Rhodes said. "I appreciate it."

"They're good boys," Mrs. Appleby said, as if she were

trying to convince herself as much as Rhodes. "Are you sure you can't stay and have a piece of that chicken? There's a drumstick left, for sure."

Rhodes could almost taste the batter on the drumstick, but he said, "I wish I could, but I've got to go home. My wife's expecting me."

Mrs. Appleby smiled. She'd met Ivy. "You tell her I said hello."

"I'll do that," Rhodes said.

6

▼

IT HAD TAKEN A WHILE FOR IVY TO GET USED TO RHODES'S being away from home so much at night, and Rhodes knew that she didn't like it. She'd begun to accept it as a part of his job that he could do nothing about, however.

When he got in from Obert, she had supper waiting for him. It wasn't fried chicken. It was a sandwich of sliced turkey breast on whole-wheat bread. Rhodes would have preferred bologna, but he didn't say so.

He looked in the refrigerator for something to drink. He was hoping for Dr Pepper, but he knew there wouldn't be any. There were skim milk and grape juice.

He chose the milk.

Ivy sat at the table with him while he ate. "I've been thinking," she said.

"About what?"

"You know. About Lige Ward. Do you want to know what I think happened?"

Rhodes was agreeable. "Sure. You mean you already know who killed him?"

"What if Press Yardley and Mrs. Ward were having an affair? Did you think about that?"

Rhodes took a drink of milk. It was cold, but it didn't have much taste. He set the glass back on the table.

"It never entered my mind," he said.

"I don't know why not. Mrs. Ward's not that old, and I can imagine what it was like around that house. Lige was really bitter about having to close his store, and he probably took it out on her. She might've wanted to talk to someone about it, and Press Yardley was right there. Sometimes a sympathetic listener can become more than just a listener."

Rhodes took a bite of the sandwich, which had a little more taste to it than the milk. It would've been even better with a few spoonfuls of Miracle Whip on it, but Ivy thought that Miracle Whip had too much fat in it. Rhodes had tried the new nonfat Miracle Whip, and he hated it. So now he was eating his sandwiches with mustard. He didn't much like mustard, but without it the turkey tasted a little like typing paper.

"Press Yardley doesn't strike me as the sympathetic type," Rhodes said after he finished chewing.

"You can't ever tell," Ivy said. "You probably don't seem like the sympathetic type to some people, but I know better."

"So Press Yardley got to know Rayjean Ward and then killed Lige for love?"

Ivy grinned. "Either that, or he caught him stealing his emus."

On the whole, Rhodes liked the second theory a lot better.

The telephone rang just as Rhodes was finishing the sandwich. It was Hack.

"Dr. White's all done. He's still at Ballinger's, if you want to talk to him."

"Call him back," Rhodes said. "Tell him I'm on the way. Tell him I'll meet him in Ballinger's office."

*　*　*

Ivy turned down the chance to go to Ballinger's with Rhodes, not that he blamed her. Whatever he found out, it wasn't going to be pleasant.

Dr. White was sitting in Ballinger's office, and when Rhodes walked in, the funeral director was regaling White with an account of autopsies he'd read about in mystery novels.

"It seems to me that every single time a cop goes to a morgue, there's some guy in there eating a sandwich. Did you ever do anything like that, Doc? Eat a sandwich while an autopsy was going on?"

"I'm usually a little too busy for that," Dr. White said.

"Yeah, but what about somebody who's helping you? Or one of the witnesses to the autopsy? Did any of *them* ever eat a sandwich?"

White shook his head. "Not that I can remember."

"That's what I figured. Those writers just put stuff like that in their books to gross people out. I've worked on clients here for twenty-five years, and I've never eaten a thing while I'm on the job. And I wouldn't allow any of my helpers to do it either. It's not sanitary."

He turned his attention to Rhodes. "Hey, Sheriff. Are you ready for the big news?"

"I'm ready," Rhodes said. "What did you find out?" he asked the doctor.

"Lige Ward was murdered," White said.

That was no surprise to Rhodes. "I figured that. How?"

"He was shot," White said. "I have the bullet for you."

"There were two wounds that I could see," Rhodes said.

"I have those bullets, too," White said. "But those aren't the bullets that killed him. The two visible wounds occurred after death. Both were from shots fired at very close range. The wound that killed him was in the chest. Right in the heart."

That explained the blood on Ward's shirtfront. "When did he die?" Rhodes asked.

White gave him a half-smile. "You know I don't like to give answers to questions like that. I can give you an estimate, but that's all."

"That'll have to do, then. What's the estimate?"

"I'd say somewhere between two and four o'clock this morning."

"All right. What else?"

White reached forward and pulled a notepad from Ballinger's desk. He glanced down at it before he spoke again.

"He'd been drinking before he was shot. And he might have been in a fight. There's a large bruise on his chest that's unrelated to the gunshot wound. It's on the opposite side."

"Is that the only bruise?"

"Yes, but there're some scratches on his arms. I can't tell what made the scratches. There was nothing in the wounds that I could identify." White flipped through his notes. "That's about all I can tell you."

"Was he moved?"

"From where?"

"I don't know," Rhodes said. "What I mean is, was he shot somewhere else and moved into the outhouse?"

Dr. White looked thoughtful. After a few seconds he said, "Probably. But he wasn't moved far. The way the blood pooled in the body indicates that he was sitting on the seat for most of the time after his death. I wish I could tell you more, but that's it."

"What about the wounds?" Rhodes said. "Could they have been self-inflicted?"

"There were traces of gunpowder on his hand, but that might mean only that his hand was close to the gun when it went off. I wish I could do better for you, but that's all I can say."

"That's a start," Rhodes said. He looked at Ballinger. "What about Mrs. Ward? Has she been in?"

"She and her sister came in and made the funeral arrangements, but she hasn't seen Lige yet. I'll have to get him ready tonight, and she can see him tomorrow."

"What time is she coming in?"

"Sometime in the morning. There's no rush. Do you need to talk to her?"

"I'll see her at home," Rhodes said.

The next day at the jail, Hack told Rhodes that Ferrin and his friends had been bonded out. Rhodes would have liked to question them again, but he had their addresses. He had other things to work on first.

Ruth Grady stopped in and showed Rhodes the casts she'd made at Yardley's emu pens.

"I've got all the fingerprints from that portable toilet, too," she said. "There's a jillion of them—all over the door, all over the walls, everywhere. Did you open the door?"

Rhodes admitted that he had.

"Then I've probably got yours. I don't think there's any help there."

"What about the casts?"

"If you didn't walk by the gate, then we may have something."

"Nobody walked by the gate," Rhodes said. "I asked them not to."

"Good. There are some prints of Yardley's shoes, but there was another set there. And somebody'd been walking around there in boots."

"You'd better go down to Ballinger's and take a cast of Lige Ward's shoes. I wouldn't be surprised if there were a match," Rhodes said.

As soon as Ruth had left, Hack, who had his Watchman tuned in to "Good Morning America," gave Rhodes a report on what he'd found out about Press Yardley's neighbor.

"That Nard King doesn't have any record. Just a couple of traffic tickets in Dallas."

Rhodes didn't think that was much help. Anyone driving a truck in Dallas was likely to have traffic tickets.

"What about the portable toilet?" he asked.

"Sani-Can don't open till nine, but I don't think we'll have to call 'em. I think I can already tell you where that porta-potty came from."

"Where's that?" Rhodes asked.

Hack, as was often the case, didn't answer the question immediately. He had to lead up to it.

"I got a call early this mornin' from Joe Bates."

He looked at Rhodes as if he expected the sheriff to know who Joe Bates was, but Rhodes had no idea.

"Joe Bates," Hack said. "He runs Bates Construction with his daddy."

"Oh," Rhodes said. "And?"

"And he said that when he got out to the worksite this mornin', he was missin' a porta-potty. Said some son of a gun musta stole it."

"Where was the construction site?" Rhodes asked.

"That's the interestin' part," Hack said. "Joe says he's buildin' a house for a fella named Nard King."

Rhodes thought that was interesting, all right. "What about Lige's pickup?"

"Nothin' on that yet," Hack said. "If it's off in the woods somewhere, we may never find it. It'll just rust down to the ground."

"Call Sani-Can anyway," Rhodes said. "It's nearly nine, and we'll have to make sure the one that's missing is the one that Joe Bates lost. There might be two of them on the loose; you never know."

Hack made the call while Rhodes tried to get caught up on his paperwork. He hadn't gotten much done when Hack got his attention.

"They wanta know if you got the serial number," he said.

"I didn't see one," Rhodes told him.

"Well, they gotta have it to make the identification."

Hack turned back to the phone and talked, then faced Rhodes again. "It's not on the front with the name. It's on the back."

"I'll have to check it. You get the number of the one Bates is leasing."

Hack spoke into the phone and then took down a number.

"Five-six-six-seven-four," he said.

Rhodes got up and took the piece of paper. "Did you tell them that they might not be getting their toilet back for a while?"

"Yeah. Bates'd already called 'em about replacin' the one he needs out at King's. They say it's not the first time they've lost one. But they usually find 'em themselves, pretty close by the place they're missin' from. This is the first time anybody's hauled one off."

"It's probably the first time anybody's stuck a body in one, too," Rhodes said.

"I'd bet on that," Hack said. "What're you gonna do now?"

"First I'm sending the slugs Dr. White took out of Lige to the forensics lab to see what caliber they are."

Rhodes had already looked them over. They were tagged in separate bags, but they all looked like .38s to him. He wanted to find out if the ones in the wounds inflicted after death had come from the same pistol as the ones in the wall of the Sani-Can, which he was also sending. If they had, that would mean that two of the shots fired by Ferrin and his buddies had gone through the wall and into Lige. He would also have to send the pistol to make the match conclusive.

He wasn't sure what he was hoping to find out about the third slug, the one that had killed Lige. Whatever the lab could tell him, he supposed.

And after he got the slugs and the pistol ready for mailing, he was going back to Sand Creek.

* * *

Down at Sand Creek, Rhodes saw the Sani-Can surrounded by the black-and-yellow ribbon. The door on the front still hung open, and it appeared that no one had disturbed the scene. He walked around to the back of the portable toilet, and then he could see the black numbers, which were exactly what he'd expected: 56674.

That was one mystery solved. The portable toilet had come from Nard King's place. Now all he had to do was find out how Lige Ward had gotten inside it.

Well, that and find out who'd killed Lige. And why.

It seemed as if Nard King's emu ranch was the place to start, so he drove out there. Joe Bates's crew was hammering away on the frame of the new house. There were four of them, and Rhodes walked over to see if he could tell which one was Bates.

He couldn't, so he stepped up through the skeletal wall and said to the nearest man, "Joe Bates?"

The man glanced up at Rhodes, then gestured to the left with his hammer, to where a heavyset man was nailing a crosspiece to a two-by-four. The man looked strong enough to drive a nail with one blow.

Rhodes went over, and the man stopped hammering and looked at him.

"Hey, Sheriff. You here about the Sani-Can?"

"That's right," Rhodes said. "Are you Joe Bates?"

"Sure am." Bates switched his hammer to his left hand and stuck out his right.

Rhodes shook it. Bates had a grip to match his appearance.

"I didn't think they'd send the sheriff himself just to see about a stolen toilet," Bates said when he let go of Rhodes's hand.

"There's more to it than just a stolen toilet," Rhodes said. "Where was it located?"

"Over there by the pens," Bates said, putting his hammer

into a loop on the nail apron he was wearing. "That's where we were working first, and there was no need to move it when we started on the house here. There's still a little work to do on the pens, too. Why?"

Rhodes explained as briefly as he could.

"Good Lord," Bates said when Rhodes was finished. "It's hard to believe things like that go on right here in Blacklin County. Let's go on over there, and I'll show you right where it was."

The location was right beside the gravel drive that led from the road to King's emu pens. There wouldn't be any useful tracks on the gravel.

"Be easy enough to drive in here off the road and tip that can into a pickup, I guess," Bates said.

Rhodes thought so too. There was a gate at the road, but it seemed as if King never bothered to close it. Maybe with only four emus, he didn't think he had much to lose. And maybe he'd had only two emus until a couple of nights ago.

He wondered why King hadn't heard anything when the outhouse was being stolen, but then he thought about the noisy air conditioner. If King slept with the air conditioner running, he wouldn't be able to hear much of anything that went on outside the house.

"Sani-Can's bringing us out another portable this morning," Bates said. "We could probably use the toilet in the house if we had to."

"Is King in there?" Rhodes asked.

"Haven't seen him today, but I guess he's in there. He usually comes out sooner or later to see how we're doing."

"I'll go talk to him, then," Rhodes said. "Thanks for your help."

"Don't mention it. Just wish I could tell you something useful."

Rhodes watched Bates go back to his framing, then knocked on King's door. King answered at once.

"Good morning, Sheriff. You come about those bills of sale?"

"That's right," Rhodes said. He noticed that the air conditioner was still banging away. "Do you have them?"

"As a matter of fact, I don't," King said. "Can't put my hand on 'em for some reason. I'm looking, though."

King didn't seem as nervous as he had the previous evening. And he didn't invite Rhodes to come inside. Rhodes wondered if he'd called an attorney. Or maybe he'd just been thinking about how hard emus were to identify.

"I'd like to see the bills of sale as soon as I could," Rhodes said.

"Am I being charged with anything?"

"No. But two emus were stolen. It would be a good idea for you to be able to prove you didn't do it."

"I thought it worked the other way," King said. " 'Innocent until proven guilty.' "

"That's the way it works, all right," Rhodes said. "It's just that there's murder involved now."

"Murder?"

"Lige Ward," Rhodes said. "He was murdered."

King looked surprised. "Murdered? Who did it?"

"I'll find out," Rhodes said. He decided not to tell King where Lige's body had been found. At least not yet. "Now what about those bills of sale?"

"I'll look," King said, trying to appear as if he meant it. "I'll give you a call if I find them."

And that was all Rhodes could get out of him. It was evident that there was something King was trying to hide, but Rhodes wasn't quite sure what it was. Emus had to be part of it, but was that all?

As Rhodes left, the Sani-Can truck was driving up with a new portable toilet. Rhodes waited until they had set it up, nearer to the house this time, and then drove over to Lige Ward's place to talk to Rayjean. Now that he was certain that Lige had been murdered, there were a few more questions he had to ask her, such as who Lige's enemies were, and what his relationships with Yardley and King had been.

The guineas called raucously as Rhodes drove up to the house, scattering in front of his car like balloons blown in the wind. He was sure they'd alert anyone in the house.

But Rayjean wasn't at home. Rhodes knocked loudly on the door, but no one answered. Rayjean's car, a five-year-old Ford, was parked at the side of the house, but Rhodes thought she'd probably gone into town with her sister.

He tried the doorknob, and it turned easily. That was a little strange, but it wasn't exactly unusual. There were still people in the country who didn't lock their doors when they went into town. And Rayjean might have been distracted by Lige's death.

Rhodes didn't go inside. He had no reason to search the house. But since there was no one around, he thought he might search somewhere else.

It wasn't far to the woods. He could walk there in a few minutes, and if there was any sign of a cockfight, it shouldn't be too hard to find.

There were ruts running through the pasture toward the woods, and Rhodes supposed that Lige occasionally drove there to feed the five or six head of cattle that idly watched Rhodes walking along the ruts toward the trees.

The sun was getting high, but it was shady and cool under the trees, elms and hackberry mostly, with a few pecans and oaks, too. There was even a big hickory-nut tree.

A squirrel chattered overhead and rustled through the leaves as it jumped from one tree to the next. The shaking of the limbs disturbed a blue jay that complained loudly.

Rhodes hadn't gone more than fifty yards into the woods when he saw the clearing ahead, and in the clearing was the cockpit.

It wasn't much, nothing more than a crude ring of boards held in place by pegs driven into the ground. There were a couple of old aluminum lawn chairs sitting nearby, with their green plastic webbing sagging and torn. Most people would probably bring their own chairs, or simply stand.

On the other side of the pit was a pickup, Lige Ward's beyond a doubt. It had a camper cap on it; Hack hadn't mentioned that, but it wouldn't have been in the information he found in the computer.

There was one other thing. Rhodes didn't notice it at first, but then he saw it, lying in the middle of the ring.

Rhodes couldn't quite see exactly what it was, but he started running all the same.

When he got to the ring, he could see all too well. At first it had looked like a pile of dirty laundry, but it wasn't that.

It was Rayjean Ward, and she was just as dead as her husband.

7

FOR JUST A SECOND, EVERYTHING STOPPED. RHODES COULD no longer hear the squirrel or the blue jay. Even the wind disappeared, and the leaves on the trees seemed frozen in place. It was as if someone had thrown a switch and stopped time.

Then the switch was flipped again and all the sounds flooded back, but there was one other sound, something that Rhodes hadn't heard earlier.

Someone had started running through the woods, rustling dead leaves, cracking dry sticks underfoot, and causing a jay to flutter up through the trees, squawking in disgust.

Rhodes ran across the cockpit and took off toward the noises, which were receding in the direction of a dirt road that cut through the woods and went on into Obert. Rhodes wasn't sure who owned the land on the other side of the road, but it didn't matter. What mattered was catching up to whoever was running away.

Rhodes didn't know that he could catch anyone, however. He was already panting, and he knew that the road was probably a half mile away, maybe a little farther. He wondered if the exercise bike that he pedaled whenever he thought about it was doing him any good at all.

He put his arm up to ward off the branches that were trying to whip across his eyes, but in worrying about his eyes he forgot about his feet. A nimble green vine with tiny thorns snaked up through the dead leaves on the ground and wrapped itself around his ankle, sending him sprawling.

Rhodes barely had time to yell. Then he landed hard and slid about a foot through dead sticks and leaf mold. The vine tore at his socks and scratched his shoes and broke loose just as he came to a stop. He lay there on the ground for a second or two, smelling dirt and trying to catch his breath. His blood was rushing in his ears and he could no longer hear the person he had been pursuing.

He sat up and assessed the damages. There didn't seem to be anything permanent, but he was sure he would have a few bruises to show. As his breathing returned to normal, he realized that he still could no longer hear anyone else in the woods.

He reached out, grabbed a low-hanging limb, and used it to pull himself up. He continued to listen, but he still heard nothing unusual.

Did that mean that whoever he'd been chasing had already made it to the road? Impossible, he decided, unless he'd been chasing an Olympic sprinter. He was slow, but he wasn't *that* slow.

Rhodes looked through the trees ahead of him. That's all there was—trees. There was no sign of anyone else in the woods at all. Had he only imagined that he'd heard someone?

No, he'd heard something, all right, not much question about that.

Another thought occurred to Rhodes. What if the person he'd been chasing was just as winded as he was? Whoever it was might have heard Rhodes fall and taken the opportunity to catch his breath.

Might have heard. That was a laugh. He would have to be deaf not to have heard. Rhodes had probably sounded like a derailed locomotive engine plowing along the ground.

Rhodes stood silently and listened. Still nothing. He started moving as quietly as he could through the trees. He wasn't exactly as silent as an experienced woodsman. The Deerslayer would have scoffed at him, Rhodes was sure, and whoever was hiding up there ahead, if anybody was, was probably scoffing too.

And probably waiting to jump out from behind a tree and do away with Rhodes just as he'd done away with Rayjean Ward, though Rhodes didn't see any trees that really looked big enough to conceal anyone.

He was cautious nevertheless, and it therefore came as a big surprise when someone landed on his back and bore him to the ground even harder than the first time he'd fallen.

He had been careful to look behind the trees, but he hadn't thought about looking *up*.

He didn't have time to be disgusted with himself, however. He was too busy trying to catch his breath and to buck the heavy weight off his back.

He inhaled part of a scratchy dry leaf and started to cough, but the cough was cut off when something hard smacked him across the back of the head. After that his eyes wouldn't focus right, and his mind went blank for a while.

When Rhodes came to, he hardly noticed the pain in the back of his head. What he noticed was that he could hear someone running through the trees again. Whoever it was, he wasn't any more of a woodsman than Rhodes. He was making as much noise as a rogue buffalo.

Rhodes knew he had to get back in the chase. He shook himself and stood up.

Then he fell right back down. In the last fall, he had twisted his right ankle, and the pain felt as if someone were hitting him on the ankle bone with a short iron rod.

He got up again, more carefully, and hobbled forward. For the first time he thought of his .38 revolver. He never liked to use a gun when he didn't know at whom he was shooting. There was always the chance he might shoot someone who didn't deserve it.

This seemed like a special circumstance, however, so he drew the pistol from the holster he wore in the small of his back and fired a shot into the tops of the trees.

"Stop," Rhodes croaked, feeling like a fool. He coughed up the leaf fragment that had lodged in the back of his throat and spit it out. "Stop, or I'll shoot."

The runner didn't stop. He started moving even faster, if anything.

"Damn," Rhodes said, putting the .38 back in the holster and stumbling forward, wincing every time his right foot touched the ground.

He was able to keep going, however, and he was within twenty yards of emerging from the trees when he heard a car door slam and an engine start.

He cleared the last of the trees just in time to see a car pulling away, dust swirling around it. It was a black Cadillac Fleetwood. Just like the one Brother Alton drove.

The walk back to the cockpit was slow, but Rhodes was convinced that his ankle was getting better already. All he had to do was walk on it a little and keep it limber.

Rayjean Ward was still there when he got back. She was lying on her side with one hand underneath her head, as if she had just lain down for a nap. Rhodes didn't stop to examine her any more closely. He hobbled on back toward the house. He had to get to a telephone.

*　*　*

After he made his phone calls, he searched the house. There wasn't anything that looked like a clue. There was the big TV set and a VCR, and in the kitchen there were quite a few other electronic gadgets—a microwave oven, a bread-maker, a juicer—which Rhodes thought were probably mementos of Ward's final days in the hardware store.

The refrigerator held things that made Rhodes's mouth water. Whole milk. Cheddar cheese. There was even a half gallon of Blue Bell Homemade Vanilla in the freezer compartment. Things Ivy wouldn't let in the house. The peanut butter was in a built-in pantry. Rhodes thought for a second about having a sandwich, but he didn't. He was even more tempted by the package of Oreos, but he resisted those, too.

In the garage there was a neatly laid-out workshop, with a table saw, a router, and some other woodworking tools. On one wall there were several rods and reels hanging from hooks. They were all covered with fine wood dust, and Rhodes wondered if Ward had ever used them. Rhodes hoped he had.

There was also a dusty filing cabinet that contained most of Ward's old business papers but nothing of any interest to Rhodes.

He went back into the house and searched the bedrooms and bathroom. There were clothes in the closets and dressers, the usual toilet articles and non-prescription drugs in the bathroom. The only thing Rhodes thought was out of the ordinary was a Victoria's Secret catalog in one of the dresser drawers, which otherwise held only four plain white cotton nightgowns, and for some reason looking at it made him feel even sadder about Rayjean Ward than he had at first.

He put everything back as it had been except the catalog, which he stuck deep into a black plastic bag that lined a trash can under the kitchen sink. He pushed it under old newspapers and orange rinds where he was sure that Rayjean's sister would never see it. Then he went back outside and drove down to the cockpit. His ankle was still hurting, and he didn't feel much like walking.

By the time the ambulance had come and gone and the JP had done his duty, Rhodes had gone over the cockpit thoroughly. He hadn't found anything of interest there either, however.

He had also looked over Lige Ward's pickup. There was nothing of interest in the cab, but the camper was littered with feathers that looked a lot like the one Rhodes had picked up at Ballinger's the previous evening. There didn't seem to be much doubt that Ward had been hauling some kind of fowl in his truck, and Rhodes was convinced that the fowl had been emus. He would have Dr. Slick come to examine the truck just to make certain.

He went back into the Wards's house and called Slick, who confirmed that the feather Rhodes had given him had come from an emu, and Rhodes told him about the truck.

"Don't worry about the yellow ribbon," Rhodes said. "Just walk right under it and look in the pickup camper. Anytime today will be all right."

Slick said he'd try to get there but that he had a lot of sick cats coming in that morning. "Some kind of virus. They just lie around all day like wet noodles."

Rhodes said, "I thought cats did that all the time anyway."

"You might have a point there," Slick admitted. "But the owners of these cats are mighty upset."

Rhodes told him that the camper was important, and Slick said that he'd stop by after his office hours if he couldn't get away before then. Rhodes thanked him and hung up the phone.

It was time to pay a visit to Brother Alton and the Free Will Church of the Lord Jesus.

* * *

Brother Alton's full name and title—The Reverend Alton Downey—were painted in flaking black letters on a lopsided sign in front of the church building located just outside the Clearview city limits.

The building itself wasn't in much better shape than the sign. It hadn't been painted in a good many years. It sat on concrete blocks and leaned slightly to Rhodes's left as he faced the front door. The black composition shingles were peeling off the top of the steeple, and one of the windows had a missing pane that had been replaced by a piece of cardboard held in place by silvery strips of duct tape.

Brother Alton's car was parked on the shady side of the building near the entrance to a small room that jutted out from the side and which looked as if it had been added as an afterthought.

The afterthought was Brother Alton's office. There was a set of prefab concrete steps in front of the unpainted door, and Rhodes mounted them before he knocked.

"Come in," Brother Alton called from inside.

The doorknob hung uselessly in its socket, but Rhodes gave it a couple of turns for luck before pushing open the door.

Brother Alton sat behind an old desk coated with dark varnish that was peeling off in long strips. There was no electricity in the room; the only light came in through the dirt-streaked windows. Pages of paper, some of them crumpled, covered the desktop, and a large leather-covered Bible lay open in front of the preacher, who looked up at Rhodes through his rimless glasses.

"Good morning, Sheriff," Brother Alton said, looking quickly back down.

"Working on your sermon?" Rhodes asked.

Brother Alton didn't look up again. "Um, yes. Working on my sermon. My little flock is eager for the Word."

Rhodes had to take only a step from the door to the desk.

He put a finger on the open Bible. "Anything in there about cockfights?"

"Um, cockfights? That's . . . um . . . a topic that the Lord's Word don't have much to say about. What're you askin' that for?"

Brother Alton made the mistake of glancing up as he phrased the question and found Rhodes looking right into his eyes. The preacher's right hand twitched nervously and knocked one of the crumpled papers across the desk. It fell to the floor at Rhodes's feet.

Rhodes picked up the paper and smoothed it out. "Jesus spoke to that sinful woman at the well," he read aloud. "And he told her all about her whole iniquitous life." Rhodes stopped reading and put the paper on the desk. "Have you been to see any sinful women today, Brother Alton?"

"God knows," Brother Alton sighed. "God knows."

"He's not the only one that knows," Rhodes said. "I saw your car. How old are you, anyway?"

"How . . . huh?"

"How old? I wouldn't ever have thought to look up in that tree for you."

"God forgive me," Brother Alton said. "I surely didn't want to do that, Sheriff."

"I wish you hadn't," Rhodes said. "You made me twist my ankle."

Brother Alton sighed again. "I'm surely sorry. I didn't mean to hurt you."

"You shouldn't have run."

"I know that. But you don't know how it felt, walking up on a dead woman like that. She was an awful sight, lyin' there in that ring. And then to have the sheriff come up on me. How was I to know what you might think? I was afraid that you might believe I had somethin' to do with killin' her, so I ran. And then when you fell down—"

Brother Alton looked at Rhodes. "Are you sure you

didn't hurt your ankle then? Instead of when I jumped on you?"

"I'm sure," Rhodes told him.

"Well, then, I'm mighty sorry for hurtin' you. Anyway, when you fell down, I thought maybe I could stop and get my breath, but you got up so quick and came after me that I was still blowin' like a bellows. I was afraid you'd catch up to me sure. So I climbed up in that tree and jumped on you. It wasn't very high."

Rhodes reached up and touched the knot on the back of his head. "Jumping on me's not all you did."

"God forgive me," Brother Alton said, shaking his head from side to side. "God forgive me."

"What did you hit me with, anyway?" Rhodes asked.

Brother Alton stopped moving his head. "Just a little old hick'ry limb. I didn't hit you very hard."

"Hard enough," Rhodes said.

"Lord knows. Lord knows."

"Let's leave the Lord out of this," Rhodes said. "What were you doing at that cockpit?"

"I'd heard about the fights that Lige was havin'," Brother Alton said. "I wanted to see if it was true."

Rhodes shook his head. It seemed as if everyone in the county had heard about the cockfights except him.

"What if it was?"

"If it was, then I was goin' to have a talk with Miz Ward. She'd called and asked me to preach Lige's funeral, and I didn't know if I could do that with Lige havin' a sin like that on his account. I didn't want people thinkin' I was tryin' to gloss anything over."

Rhodes wondered whether Brother Alton was more worried about Lige or about what people would think about their preacher.

"You could've gone in the front way," he said. "Why didn't you do that?"

Brother Alton brushed at the shoulder of his suit jacket.

There was a piece of a leaf there that Rhodes hadn't noticed before. The leaf fell onto the top of the desk.

"I didn't want to just go right up to Miz Ward and accuse her husband of anything that wasn't the truth," the preacher said, "him bein' dead and all. I thought I'd just check it out first without her seein' me."

"And you found Mrs. Ward in the woods?"

"Just like you saw her. She was lyin' there dead." He looked out the little window and back at Rhodes. "I heard you comin' and ducked back in the trees. Then I just started to run. I shouldn't've done that. I shouldn't've run. But I didn't kill her, Sheriff."

Rhodes had never thought of Brother Alton as a killer, and he said as much. Then he asked, "Did you see anyone else when you were coming along through the woods?"

"Not a soul. Whoever killed her was long gone by the time I got there."

"Were you planning to call me, by any chance? Let me know there was a dead body out there?"

"I didn't think about it, to tell the truth," Brother Alton admitted. "All I wanted to do was get out of there. I've seen dead people before, plenty of 'em, but they've all been in hospitals or funeral homes. That's the first time I ever saw one dead in the woods like that."

"What about when you got back here?"

"I was goin' to call, but I got started workin' on my sermon. It sorta calms me down to do that. I needed a lot of calmin' down."

Brother Alton's head shook, and then the shaking moved down to his shoulders and chest. He put his hands down flat on the desk, and the shaking stopped.

"I guess I'm not calmed down yet," he said. "But I never killed anybody, Sheriff. And I never meant to cause you any trouble. I just got scared."

Rhodes thought the preacher was telling the truth. Murder was enough to spook anyone, and he didn't blame

Brother Alton for being a little afraid of the consequences of finding a corpse.

But he was the sheriff, after all, so he said, "It's a crime not to report a body. You know that, don't you?"

Brother Alton half-rose from his chair. "You aren't gonna arrest me, are you? I've never been in any trouble, Sheriff. I've never done anything against the law."

"I'm not going to arrest you, but if you think of anything else you saw out there, something you can't remember right now, you'd better call."

Brother Alton sank back into his chair in relief. "I'll call, Sheriff, you can count on that. I know I've done wrong, and I'll try to make amends."

Rhodes left the office wondering if Brother Alton's humbling experience would affect his preaching. If the pastor hadn't identified with his flock's secret wrongdoings before, he could certainly do so now.

Rhodes was afraid that it wouldn't make much difference; things didn't generally work out that way. By tomorrow, Brother Alton, if he was like most people, would probably have convinced himself that he had done nothing wrong at all.

8

BETTY EVERS WAS ABOUT FIVE YEARS OLDER THAN HER SISTER
Rayjean and looked a lot like her, except that her hair was
cut short and dyed a deep black.

She didn't take the news about Rayjean's death well at
all, and Rhodes was glad he'd thought to call Ruth Grady
on the radio and get her to meet him at Betty's house before
giving her the news.

Betty's husband had died of a heart attack two years
previously, and now she'd lost her brother-in-law and her
sister on successive days. It was no wonder that she was
almost in a state of shock.

She was, however, able to tell Rhodes and Grady that
Rayjean had no more enemies than a newborn calf and that
Rayjean, like Lige, had been universally liked in Clearview
and Obert.

"It's gangs," she said. "It must be gangs, coming in from
outside, selling dope and causing trouble."

Rhodes had dealt with that kind of thing before, in a
small way, and he didn't think that was the case this time,
but Betty Evers couldn't offer any better explanation.

Rhodes left Ruth with her in case she thought of something else, but he didn't hold out much hope that that would

happen. There was a motive for the killings; there always was. But it looked as if it was going to take a while to find out what it was.

Rhodes drove back to the jail to make his report. He wondered just what the death of Rayjean Ward had to do with that of her husband. It seemed obvious that the two deaths were related, but for the life of him Rhodes couldn't figure out how, and Rayjean's sister had been no help at all.

Ward's pickup full of feathers offered pretty good circumstantial evidence that Ward had been rustling emus. That fact could possibly connect him with both Nard King and Press Yardley, though there was no proof that King had received stolen emus from Ward, just as there was no proof that Ward had stolen part of Yardley's flock.

And even if all those things were somehow connected, there was no reason why Rayjean Ward should be any part of them. It was true that Rhodes could easily enough believe that Lige would resort to holding cockfights to raise money, and there was no way that Rayjean could have been unaware of it, since the fights were held almost within sight of her house. But at the same time Rhodes couldn't see Mrs. Ward as having any part in stealing emus. Cockfighting was one thing. There were plenty of people who didn't see anything wrong with it, didn't believe it should be against the law. Rayjean Ward might have been one of those people. Theft was something else.

It was a little like the filed gaff that had been in Lige's clothing. Cockfighters were engaging in an illegal activity, but they had a code of their own. There were limits to what they would do, though the limits were generally defined by how much they could get away with. Still, they wouldn't like it if someone was using a gaff like the one Rhodes had found.

Reflecting on the gaff, Rhodes had another thought. What if Lige had been doing more than simply organizing the cockfights? What if he had been taking part in them?

What if someone had caught him using the filed gaff and confronted him? There might very well have been a fight that ended in Lige's death. A fight would at least explain the bruise on Ward's chest.

Rhodes parked in front of the jail without reaching any conclusions. He had to find out a lot more about a lot of things before he did that.

Hack was watching the little TV set when Rhodes walked in. Lawton was looking over his shoulder. Rhodes strolled over for a glimpse of the program that had them so engrossed.

"What's that?" Rhodes asked.

The jailer and the dispatcher looked up sharply. They hadn't heard Rhodes come in.

Hack reached out and switched the TV set off. "Nothin'," he said. There was a shifty look in his eyes.

"It was 'All My Children,' " Rhodes said. "I recognized Susan Lucci."

"Who?" Lawton asked.

"She plays Erica," Rhodes told him.

"Who's Erica?" Hack asked.

"There's nothing wrong with watching soap operas," Rhodes said. "You don't have to be ashamed of it, as long as you get your work done."

"We weren't watchin' it," Lawton said. "We were just flippin' through the channels, seein' what was on."

Rhodes nodded. "Right."

"Besides," Hack said, "we got a lot more things to worry about than some soap opera."

"Like murder," Rhodes suggested.

"There's that, all right," Hack agreed. "Sure was a shame about Miz Ward. You know who did it yet?"

"I don't have any idea."

"Well, you better be gettin' one," Lawton said.

Hack glared at him. Hack liked to think that he was in

charge of the conversation; he didn't like it when Lawton tried to horn in.

Lawton glared back. He thought he had just as much right as Hack to impart information to the sheriff.

"Why don't you tell me what's going on instead of trying to stare each other down," Rhodes suggested.

"We're not starin'," Hack said. "Not me, anyway."

Rhodes waved a hand dismissively. "Never mind that. Just tell me what's on your minds."

"There's nothin' on our minds," Hack said.

"Just that woman," Lawton said, giving Rhodes a look. "He thinks about that woman all the time."

Hack started to get up. "I'm tired of you talkin' about Miz McGee that way."

Lawton's face was bland. "What way?"

"You know what way. I'm tired of it."

Rhodes was tired of the whole conversation. "Let's forget Hack's love life and get back to the beginning of this. Why had I better be getting an idea about who killed the Wards?"

"Love life," Lawton said. "That's a good one."

Rhodes regretted his choice of words. "You know what I mean. Now what did you two have to tell me?"

Hack sank back in his chair. "You're gonna have a visitor," he said.

"Who?" Rhodes asked.

"That's the good part," Lawton said. "You'll be real glad to see him."

Rhodes could tell by Lawton's gleeful tone that he wasn't going to be glad at all.

"Who?" he asked again.

"Well," Hack said, "he's got red hair."

Rhodes groaned inwardly. "Red Rogers."

"The one and only," Lawton said.

"He called about ten minutes before you got here," Hack

said. "He wants the whole story about how Blacklin
County's becomin' a hotbed of rooster fightin' and murder."

Rhodes walked over to his own desk and sat down. "He
really said that? 'A hotbed'?"

Hack nodded. "That's what he said, all right. It'll sound
real good on the five-o'clock news."

Rhodes groaned again, audibly this time.

"Just a fella tryin' to do his job," Lawton said reassur-
ingly.

"I know," Rhodes said, and he did. He just didn't like
Rogers's job.

Red Rogers was the nearest thing Blacklin County had to
a media personality. His real name was Larry Redden, and
he had a daily four-hour country-music show on the local
radio station. He also did all the news broadcasts and the
"Saturday Trading Post," on which anyone in what he
grandly called the "Tri-County Area" could offer goods to
swap.

His most recent undertaking, however, was a weekly talk
show in the manner of Rush Limbaugh. The talk show was
what bothered Rhodes. While Rogers was more than willing to take on world and national politics, offering his pat
solutions to any and all problems (cut all foreign aid, allow
every citizen to carry a handgun, let the poor fend for
themselves, et cetera), he didn't limit himself to the big
picture. All too often, from Rhodes's point of view at any
rate, Rogers ranted about purely local issues, sometimes
about things that involved the sheriff's office.

What happened as a result was entirely predictable. The
county commissioners got nervous and, being elected offi-
cials, they immediately began looking for someone either to
blame or to hold responsible.

In the sheriff's office, they didn't have to look far.

Only two weeks previously, Rogers had uncovered what
he considered a hideous scandal. Sheriff Dan Rhodes, he

announced on his show, was using county vehicles for private transportation.

It was true that Rhodes often visited his home in the county car and that he drove it to and from work. But, as Rhodes pointed out to the commissioners, it made sense for him to do so. Otherwise, when he got a call at home, he would have to drive to the jail and get the county car before going out on a call. The extra time that would take could be crucial in plenty of situations, and it wasn't as if he were driving to fancy restaurants in Dallas or dance clubs in Houston on county gasoline.

The commissioners agreed that Rhodes had a point, and he continued to drive the car with the admonition that he'd better never be caught going to the grocery store in it.

"I never have gone anywhere like that in it," Rhodes told them.

"And you'd better not start," they said.

None of that really satisfied Red Rogers, but he was distracted the next week by the fact that one of Clearview's trash pick-up men had been paid an extra fifty dollars one month, thanks to a clerical error. What enraged Rogers wasn't the error; it was the fact that the man hadn't paid back the fifty dollars immediately. It had taken him two weeks.

Rhodes felt sorry for the trash pick-up man, but he was glad that Rogers's attention was at least momentarily distracted from the sheriff's office.

But now Rogers would be back. The fact that the Wards's deaths would get a big play on the news didn't matter to Rhodes. By now, half the population of Blacklin County had heard about that. You didn't need a radio to get the news in a small place like Clearview. What mattered, however, was that Rogers would no doubt play up the murders on his talk show, thereby putting pressure on Rhodes and on the commissioners. It wasn't going to make finding the killer any easier.

Rhodes stood up. "I think I'd better go do a little investigating," he said.

The door to the office swung open.

"Too late," Hack said.

"Too late for what?" Red Rogers asked, stepping into the room.

He was wearing a pair of gray Levi's Dockers, a white cotton shirt, and a pair of white-soled deck shoes. And he was carrying his tape recorder.

"Too late for me to be hangin' around here," Lawton said. "I've got to check on those cells."

He went out the back door, leaving Hack and Rhodes to deal with Rogers.

"And I've got to check on these serial numbers," Hack said, turning to his computer.

Rhodes was on his own.

Rogers smiled broadly, then turned on his radio voice. "Well, Sheriff, it looks as if we've got ourselves a real hotbed of trouble here."

Rhodes looked over Rogers's shoulder at Hack, who was staring at the computer screen. "Hotbed?"

"You know what I mean, Sheriff," Rogers said, switching on the recorder. "On the record now, what's this about a vicious criminal ring of fowl abusers running amok in the county?"

"Foul abusers?"

"F-o-w-l. Fowl."

"As in cockfighting?" Rhodes asked.

"That's exactly what I mean," Rogers said. "Dead animal carcasses littering the countryside to satisfy the brutal bloodlust of men and women little better than savages."

Rhodes thought that Rogers had spent too much time watching "Geraldo."

"I don't think there are that many carcasses around," he said. "Has anyone found one?"

"Well, no. Maybe not. But what about *human* bodies, Sheriff? Are there too many of those?"

"Even one would be too many."

"And how many do we have now? Two? One of them sadistically stuffed into a portable toilet like just another mound of human waste?"

Too much "Geraldo" and too much "Donahue," both, Rhodes thought.

"There's an investigation underway," he said.

"And I suppose we could say that you have the full resources of the department engaged in that investigation?"

"You could say that."

Rogers could hardly contain his excitement. "And I suppose you think that's just fine? To allocate all the resources of your department to solve these two murders, while the abusers of fowls have free sway to do as they please and while who knows what other crimes are being committed in the county?"

Rhodes looked at Hack again. The dispatcher's shoulders were shaking with laughter. Hack turned his head slightly and caught Rhodes's eye. He made his hand into a pistol, pointed it at his head, and pulled the trigger.

Rhodes didn't smile. He didn't think that Rogers was really all that funny.

"Do you have any helpful information, Mr. Redden?" he asked.

Rogers looked shocked at the use of his real name. He probably thought of himself as Red Rogers, having established that as his radio persona.

"I mean, Mr. Rogers," Rhodes said. "Do you have any information that might lead me to the capture and arrest of all these criminals you're talking about here?"

Rogers was indignant. "Of course not! That's not my job!"

"It's the job of every citizen to assist in the curtailment of crime," Rhodes said.

And how do you like *that* alliteration? he wondered.

"Well, of course, naturally, I know that," Rogers said, thrown off-stride. "What I meant was that it seems to me that your department has a large responsibility here, and that it might be that—"

Rhodes pressed his advantage. "Are you suggesting that it might just be that as a small, underfunded department we don't really have the resources necessary to do what's required to protect the citizens of the county? Is that what you mean? Are you suggesting a tax increase for the citizens of Blacklin County to provide for more officers and more modern equipment?"

"No, no, no," Rogers said, practically running the words together in his eagerness to get them out. Suggesting that he might favor a tax increase was tantamount to blasphemy. His listeners would lynch him in a heartbeat if he ever hinted at such a thing. "I'm simply suggesting that—"

Hack cleared his throat loudly. "Lawrence R for Raymond Redden," he said.

Rogers turned to look at the dispatcher. Rhodes could see letters glowing on the computer screen.

"No Red Rogers in the records here," Hack said. "But there's a Mr. Lawrence R for Raymond Redden, who looks to have two outstandin' tickets for exceedin' the speed limit, both issued by the DPS out on the Interstate."

Rogers clicked off the tape recorder.

"Law and order," Hack said. "Pretty important in a little town like this. Most folks pay their tickets, and they think ever'body else should, too. Makes you wonder about this Lawrence R for Raymond Redden, don't it?" He tapped the screen of the monitor with a fingernail.

Rogers's face was as red as his hair. "If you're trying to intimidate me—"

"No one's trying to do that," Rhodes said.

"Besides, that's privileged information," Rogers said. "You can't use that against me."

"Nothin' privileged about it," Hack said. "It's right there in the files for anybody who's authorized to read 'em."

"And nobody said anything about using it against you," Rhodes told him.

"You can't stop me from talking about the fowl abuse that's going on here in Blacklin County, and about the lack of response from the sheriff's department."

"No one's trying to stop you from talking," Rhodes assured him.

"Good," Rogers said. "I hope you'll tune in my show this week and see what I have to say on the subject."

"I'll try," Rhodes said. "If I get any time off from my investigation."

"Maybe you oughta do a show on the highway boys," Hack said. "On how they're always stoppin' innocent fellas for speedin'."

Rogers didn't bother to respond. He took his tape recorder and left.

Rhodes looked over at Hack. "You shouldn't have done that."

Hack grinned. "He left, didn't he?"

"True," Rhodes said. "Maybe you were right about that computer. We should've gotten it years ago."

"Tried to tell you," Hack said.

Lawton was swabbing down one of the cells when Rhodes found him. There was a strong smell of Lysol in the air.

"You get that gaff for me?" Rhodes asked.

Lawton reached into the pocket of his worn khakis and pulled out a gaff in a plastic bag. The business end of the gaff was slipped into an elongated plastic fishing bobber that covered the point and most of the filed edge.

Rhodes took the gaff and put it in his own pocket. "Now let's talk about cockfights."

Lawton leaned the mop he was wielding in a corner. "What about 'em?"

"Have you talked to Gad Pullens again? Found out who's in on it?"

"Ever'body's too closemouthed," Lawton said. "The ones I've talked to know where I work. They don't have a thing to say to me."

Rhodes nodded in understanding. "I guess I'll have to do the talking, then."

"If they won't talk to me, they ain't gonna talk to you."

"They have to. I'm the sheriff."

"Won't make any difference."

"We'll see. Where should I start?"

"You know Wally Henry?"

Rhodes already knew that Henry raised fighting cocks. "Lives down below Thurston?"

"He's the one," Lawton said. "If anybody knows anything about those fights at Lige's, he does. I haven't seen him to talk to, though, not that he'd say anything if I did."

"I'll give him a try," Rhodes said.

"I hear he don't much like it if folks go pokin' around in his private business."

"He doesn't have to like it. He just needs to help me out a little."

"He's pretty mean," Lawton said. "You remember that time five or six years back when those kids went snoopin' around his place?"

Rhodes remembered. Henry had fired off a couple of rounds of buckshot. One of the boys had wound up in the hospital getting it plucked out of his backside.

"I'd watch myself if I was you," Lawton said.

"I always do," Rhodes told him.

9

RHODES ALWAYS LIKED THE DRIVE TO THURSTON. THE ROAD was smooth, there was never much traffic, and there were still a few wildflowers growing in the thick green grass beside the road, mostly yellow daisies of some kind. Rhodes had given up on trying to learn the names of anything except bluebonnets, Indian blankets, and Indian paintbrushes. He also knew the difference between buttercups and primroses, though he hadn't admitted it to Ivy.

While he was in Thurston, he stopped at Hod Barrett's store for a Dr Pepper. The store wasn't air-conditioned, but it had a high stamped-tin ceiling with fans that stirred the air around. There were a couple of naked bulbs hanging down on wires to provide what light there was. The shelves were sparsely stocked, and Rhodes often wondered how Barrett was even getting by.

A bell rang when Rhodes pushed open the door with the fading "Rainbo Bread" ad stenciled on the screen. Hod Barrett came out from the back room and stopped when he saw Rhodes. He had never been one of the sheriff's biggest supporters.

"Can I help you, Sheriff?" he said.

"Just thought I'd stop in and have a cold drink," Rhodes said.

His ankle twinged a little as he walked over to the red-and-white Coke box and helped himself, pulling a bottle of Dr Pepper from the cold water inside.

"How much?" he asked.

"Fifty cents, includin' the tax," Barrett said, moving behind the cash register. He was so short that the top of his head barely reached the top of the register.

Rhodes dug in his pocket and came out with two quarters. He pulled a Puff from the box on the counter and wiped the water off his Dr Pepper bottle.

"You want anything to eat with that?" Barrett said. "I got sandwiches now."

"Where?" Rhodes asked, looking around.

"Back in the butcher case, keeping cool. Have a look."

Rhodes walked back to the white porcelain-enameled case and looked through the windows. There was a short row of deli sandwiches wrapped in plastic with yellow labels.

One called "The Double Stacker" caught Rhodes's eye. It had lettuce, tomatoes, two kinds of cheese, two kinds of lunch meat, mustard, and mayonnaise. He knew he should resist, but he didn't.

He pointed at it. "I'll take that one," he said.

Barrett disappeared behind the case and slid open a door. He reached in and got the sandwich. He had to stand on his tiptoes to hand it to Rhodes over the top of case.

"That'll be two ninety-seven," Barrett said.

Rhodes paid him with three ones, unwrapped the sandwich, and took a bite. It was just as good as he'd thought it would be.

"What's business like these days?" he asked when he'd finished chewing.

Barrett shook his head. "How do you think? That big grocery store by the Wal-Mart in Clearview's sucked away all my customers 'cept for the ones want a half-pound of ground meat delivered thirty minutes before their supper. And I sell a sandwich ever' now and then.''

Rhodes looked around at the half-empty shelves and thought about Lige Ward.

"I'll prob'ly have to close up in another year or two," Barrett said. "You wouldn't think it to look at the town now, but I remember when we had five grocery stores, a drugstore, two hardware stores, and even a couple of doctors and a picture show. It wasn't all that long ago, either. You can look out my front window and see all that's left of the place now."

He even sounded like Ward. Rhodes looked out the window. Barrett was right. There wasn't much to see. Most of the buildings in Thurston had been torn down and the brick sold to contractors. The buildings that still stood were deserted for the most part. Only the post office was anywhere near new, it and the bank, and Rhodes couldn't see the bank from where he stood. It wasn't in the town. It was out on the main highway.

"What brings you to town, anyway, Sheriff?" Barrett asked. "We don't see you down here much 'cept in election years."

That wasn't strictly true, but Rhodes didn't feel like getting into an argument. Hod Barrett would have enjoyed it too much. So Rhodes finished his sandwich and his Dr Pepper. He tossed the plastic sandwich wrapper in the trash can by the candy counter and stuck the bottle in the wooden case that sat by the cooler. He looked into the candy counter and was strongly tempted to buy a package of Reese's Peanut Butter Cups for dessert, but he'd already sinned enough for one day.

"I thought I might drive out and have a talk with Wally Henry," he said, straightening from the candy counter.

"I heard about Lige Ward gettin' himself killed," Barrett said. "He was fightin' roosters, wasn't he?"

"We don't know that for sure," Rhodes said, wondering who else knew about the cockfights. Maybe it had already been discussed on Red Rogers's radio show and Rhodes had missed it.

"Don't know why else anybody'd want to talk to Wally Henry 'less it was about roosters," Hod said. "Ever'body knows he raises 'em."

"Does he still live out close to Gaines Lake?"

"Yep. Been there long as I can remember."

"Does he ever come into town?"

"If he does, he don't stop here," Barrett said. "Buys his groceries in Clearview like ever'body else."

Barrett followed Rhodes outside and stood under the store's heavy wooden awning.

"Nobody cares about the place where they was born and grew up in anymore," the storekeeper said. "It don't mean any more to 'em than a hole in the ground. They wouldn't care if this place was to dry up and blow away."

Rhodes stood by his car with the door open and looked at Barrett over the top. "You're probably right," he said.

"Ain't no prob'ly to it," Barrett said.

Rhodes nodded. He got in the car and drove away.

Wally Henry lived at the top of a hill on a sandy road about a mile and a half from the highway spur that cut through the middle of Thurston. His frame house looked as if it had been designed and built by the same person who had constructed Brother Alton's church. The only hint of modernity about it was the satellite dish in the backyard. There was a green GMC pickup with rusting fenders parked under a mesquite tree near the front porch. The yard was mostly hard-packed dirt. There was an old corrugated tin barn in back of the house.

The roosters were on a patch of ground about the size of half a city block next to the house. Each one had his own open-sided triangular sheet-metal shelter about three feet high and his own food and water dish. There was grass growing between the triangular frames, but the areas patrolled by the individual roosters were like the yard—hard dirt, but neatly raked.

Each of the roosters was tethered to a metal stake driven into the ground. Obviously it wouldn't do to have them get together, and none of them showed any interest in Rhodes when he drove up.

Rhodes parked beside the GMC and got out of his car. He was about to go up on the porch and knock when Wally Henry came outside.

Henry was a big man, wide through the shoulders, with heavy arms and thick wrists. He was wearing faded jeans tucked into heavy motorcycle boots, a knit shirt that looked as if it were buttoned over a barrel, and an L.A. Raiders cap streaked with reddish dirt. He had a thick gray beard and long gray hair that he had fashioned into a pigtail as long and thick as Willie Nelson's. There was a huge wad of tobacco in his left cheek. The only small thing about him was a pair of close-set black eyes.

Henry was known around the county as a sort of outlaw, though he'd never been arrested. He had a reputation for brutishness, but no one who'd suffered at his hands had ever made a complaint. Rumor had it that they were afraid to. His major brush with the sheriff's department had been the incident mentioned by Lawton, and that complaint had been lodged by the parents of the boys, not the boys themselves. He had also been in a number of fights at the Palm Club, and once he had flattened a deputy sheriff who had been called to quell a disturbance. That had been a few years ago, and the deputy had since left the county's employ.

The game warden was even better acquainted with Henry than the sheriff's department. Since Henry had the only house for at least a mile in either direction, and since most of the land that adjoined his was owned by absentee land-

lords from Houston and Dallas, Henry felt free to roam
other people's property when they weren't around, fishing
in their stock tanks and poaching their game, primarily
out-of-season deer. Or so Rhodes had heard. As far as he
knew, none of the complaints against Henry had ever re-
sulted in so much as a fine. Maybe the landlords dropped
their complaints when they got a look at the man they were
accusing.

If Henry occasionally fished in Gaines Lake, Rhodes
didn't really blame him. The sheriff had once caught an
eight-pound largemouth bass there using live bait and a
Calcutta cane pole so limber that it took Rhodes what
seemed like an eternity to drag the fish out of the water.
That had been when you could go fishing in the lake by
paying a small fee, a dollar a day. Gaines had since closed
the lake to fishing, but Rhodes had never stopped thinking
about it.

"What can I do you fer, Sheriff?" Henry asked. He had
a clear tenor voice that was surprising from such a big man.

Rhodes walked until he was in the shade of the porch. "I
wanted to talk to you about cockfighting."

"Wouldn't know anything about that," Henry said,
crossing his arms in front of his chest and leaning against
one of the four-by-fours that supported the porch roof.
Rhodes thought he heard the nails groan in the wood. "I
just raise 'em, myself. I don't fight 'em."

"And you don't see anything wrong with that?" Rhodes
asked.

Henry pretended to think about it. "About raisin' 'em?
Nothing wrong a'tall. And it's legal, too. But I guess you
know that, you bein' the sheriff."

Henry shifted his weight and got comfortable, then sent
a stream of tobacco juice into the yard. It splattered the
ground near Rhodes's left shoe.

"Legal, but maybe not too nice for the roosters," Rhodes
suggested, ignoring the tobacco.

Henry spit again, though the stream was much smaller and fell far short of Rhodes. He wiped his mouth with the back of his hand.

"Let me tell you somethin', Sheriff," he said. He gestured toward the roosters. "Those boys out there got it a lot better than any other chickens you can think of. Plenty of food, plenty of water, nice shade, and a long life to look forward to. Compared to most chickens, they got it made."

"What about the fights?" Rhodes asked.

"What about 'em?"

"That can't be too easy on the cocks," Rhodes pointed out.

"Maybe you got the wrong idea about the fights," Henry said. "First of all, those roosters there are stags. That's what we call 'em before they're old enough to fight. When they get to fightin' age, we call 'em cocks. Maybe you didn't know that, and maybe you ain't never seen a cockfight. You prob'ly think there's always cocks gettin' killed, but they ain't. Most fights end in a decision by the referee. The cocks hardly ever get killed."

"Some of them do," Rhodes said.

Henry spit again. "Sure they do. But if you're so worried about chickens gettin' killed, you oughta be worried about the ones that're raised up for food. The ones they sell you in grocery stores and in those fried-chicken places. Those die pretty damn young.

"And then the layin' hens, they might live longer, but they're shut up in a cage all their lives, about one foot square. I've seen 'em. They don't hardly have room to turn around. Toenails grow so long they hang out the bottom of the cage till they nearly scrape the ground. Terr'ble way to live, you ask me."

"But your birds are taken care of," Rhodes said.

"Damn right. You pick up any one of 'em and give 'im a feel. Not an ounce of fat on 'im. Nothin' but the best diet for those boys. They get exercise, too. Prob'ly in better shape than you are."

Rhodes thought about how winded he'd gotten in his chase through the woods earlier. He didn't doubt that the cocks were in better shape than he was.

"You ever dope them?" he asked.

Henry straightened slowly and then came down off the porch. The wooden step creaked under his weight. He stopped right in front of Rhodes.

"What'chu mean by that?"

Henry wasn't any taller than Rhodes. Just a whole lot wider. Rhodes looked into his small black eyes.

"What I said."

Henry rocked back on his heels about a quarter of an inch, turned his head, spit. "Ever'body dopes the birds if they're fightin'. And like I said, I don't do any fightin'."

"And you don't know anyone who does."

Henry smiled. There were tobacco stains on the beard around his mouth, and his teeth were brown.

"That's right, Sheriff. I don't know anybody who does."

"If you did, what would they think about a thing like this?" Rhodes asked, bringing the plastic bag containing the gaff out of his pocket.

Henry's eyes narrowed. He knew exactly what he was looking at without a second glance, even with the plastic bobber covering most of it. "Where'd you get that?"

"I found it," Rhodes said. He held the bag up a little higher. "You want a better look at it?"

"I can see what it is."

"I wouldn't think that an honest businessman such as yourself could recognize it so easily," Rhodes said.

Henry moved his gaze from the gaff to Rhodes's face. "Are you gettin' smart with me, Sheriff?"

"I wouldn't dream of it. But I thought you didn't do any cockfighting. I guess I was just a little surprised when you recognized this gaff for what it is."

Rhodes returned the bag to his pocket. "What would you think of someone used one of those in a fight?"

"I think I'm tired of talkin' to you, that's what I think."
Henry turned and started back to the porch.

"I just have a few more questions," Rhodes said.

Henry turned slowly, twisted his mouth, and spit very
close to Rhodes's shoe. "I ain't got any more answers."

Rhodes looked down at his shoe. It was a pretty good
shoe, a Rockport, in fact, and about as comfortable as any
shoe he'd ever owned. He was glad Henry hadn't spit on it.

Rhodes didn't like fights. He didn't even like arguments.
But there was a limit to his patience.

"Don't do that again," he said.

"Do what?" Henry asked, his tiny eyes wide with inno-
cence.

"Spit," Rhodes told him. "It bothers me."

"I guess that makes us just about even. Your questions're
botherin' me. Why don't you just go on back to town and
forget about cockfights. You don't know what you're lookin' for, anyway."

Rhodes shook his head. "That's where you're wrong,"
he said. "I know what I'm looking for. I'm looking for a
man who'd kill anyone who used a gaff like that to win a
fight."

Henry reached out and with three short, thick fingers
poked Rhodes in the chest. "I don't like to be accused of
killin' anybody, Sheriff. So why don't you just get in your
little car and go on back to town where you belong?"

Rhodes brought his left forearm up and over, knocking
Henry's hand aside.

"Touching's worse than spitting," he said.

Henry snarled an unintelligible reply and swung a round-
house right that Rhodes easily avoided by taking a step
backward. He set himself for another swing, but Henry
surprised him by kicking him.

In the right ankle.

Rhodes had never realized before that the human ankle
was directly attached to all the major pain nerves in the

body, but he discovered that unsettling fact the instant Henry's boot connected.

Rhodes started to crumple, but Henry grabbed him by the front of the shirt and hauled him upright.

"Pretty sneaky for an old fart, ain't I?" Henry said, shoving Rhodes back a pace and aiming another kick, this one headed for an even more delicate spot than the injured ankle.

He missed because Rhodes was falling by the time the boot arrived. It struck him on the shoulder, and he flipped backward, landing on his shoulders and back.

Henry aimed a kick at Rhodes's head. Rhodes had seen enough Randolph Scott movies to know what to do. He had to grab Henry's foot and give it a hard wrench, thereby throwing Henry to the ground.

It didn't work for Rhodes the way it always worked in the movies. Henry's foot was moving so fast that it twisted through Rhodes's hands before the sheriff could get a grip.

By trying to grab the boot, however, Rhodes threw off Henry's aim. The boot missed Rhodes's head, but it nearly took off his ear, which immediately began throbbing and felt as if it had suddenly grown to the size of a catcher's mitt.

Rhodes scooted backward and tried to sit up. He didn't think he would mind shooting Henry if only he could get to his pistol.

He didn't have time. Henry kicked him in the chest.

Rhodes remembered the bruise on Lige Ward as he fell over and slid backward. His head hit the rear tire of the GMC.

He pushed himself up on the side of the truck and saw Henry laughing at him.

"How about it, Sheriff?" Henry taunted him. "You ready to go back to town where you belong and leave me alone out here in the country?"

Enough was enough. "You're under arrest," Rhodes

said, feeling around behind him in the pickup bed. "You have the right to remain silent. You have the right—"

"To beat the dog crap out of you," Henry said, advancing with his fists doubled.

Rhodes's hand closed around something that felt like a wooden pole. "You have the right to an attorney. You have the right—"

"To hell with that," Henry said.

Rhodes swung the pole up out of the pickup bed so fast that it seemed to whistle. Henry was taken completely by surprise, and the pole, which turned out to be a brand-new rake handle, made a very satisfactory crack when it hit him in the ribs.

"Son of a *bitch!*" Henry yelled.

"Abusive language," Rhodes said.

He rammed the end of the rake handle into Henry's breastbone as hard as he could.

"I'll . . . kill . . . you," Henry gasped, staggering backward.

"First assault, then abusive language, and now terroristic threats," Rhodes said. "You're going to be in jail for quite a while."

He jabbed Henry again, and this time the big man sat down, hard. When he tried to get up, Rhodes drew back the rake handle and said, "I've always wondered what it felt like to hit a home run."

"No," Henry said. "Had . . . enough."

"Good," Rhodes said, wondering if he was going to be able to walk to the county car and get Henry in it.

It wasn't easy, but he managed.

10

▼

"MUST'VE BEEN SOME FIGHT," HACK SAID. "WISHT I could've seen it."

"Me too," Lawton said. "What'd you hit him with, anyhow? I heard Dr. White say Wally was lucky his ribs weren't broke."

Rhodes was more worried about his own ribs, not to mention his ankle. He was walking a little better now, though, and he thought he'd be all right.

"I hit him with a rake handle," he said.

"Well, I just hope he don't sue us for police brutality," Hack said. "You're gonna have to stop bein' so rough on folks."

"Yeah," Lawton said. "I'm tired of bein' sued."

"We're not going to be sued about this," Rhodes said. "I guarantee it."

"Maybe," Hack said. "But there's a way we could be sure about that if we wanted to."

Lawton asked, "How's that?"

"TV," Hack said.

"We got us a TV already," Lawton said.

"Not that kind of TV. What we need is video cameras in all the county cars. That way, whatever happens'll be recorded on tape. If we get sued, we got the evidence of how we handled things right there for all the world to see."

"What if I'm not standing in the right place when I get hit?" Rhodes wondered.

"Sure, go ahead," Hack said. "You can pick holes in anything if you try hard enough. But lots of counties've already got cameras. City cops, too. There's already been one case of a policeman that was shot and killed, but they got the killer 'cause of the tape in his camera."

"I'm not planning to get killed," Rhodes said.

Hack laughed grimly. "Neither was he, I bet. Anyhow, you could prove that Wally Henry started that fight, or that you didn't really hurt him."

Rhodes wasn't worried about the state of Wally Henry's health or the possibility of a lawsuit, and he didn't think the county was going to spring for video cameras. He kept thinking about Henry's response to the gaff, and about the bruise on Lige Ward's chest.

"Get Ruth Grady on the radio," he told Hack. "Ask her to check around and find out if anyone saw an old GMC with rusted front fenders anywhere near Obert early this morning."

Hack got busy on the radio, and Rhodes turned to read the autopsy report on Rayjean Ward that Dr. White had left on his desk after he'd examined Wally Henry. White hadn't really pinpointed the time of death, but he was willing to say about seven o'clock, give or take an hour. Cause of death was a blow to the head.

Rhodes thought some more about Wally Henry. He thought Henry was a pretty good suspect in the deaths of both Rayjean and Lige. Now all he had to do was get him to admit it.

Henry didn't admit anything. He took the opportunity to engage in another spate of abusive language and a few more terroristic threats.

Rhodes took it all calmly. He'd heard worse.

"You might as well talk to me," he said. "I can find out if you were at the cockfights, and I can find out if you made any threats against anybody there like the ones you're making here against me."

"You can't find out a damn thing," Henry said. "And you better have those stags of mine seen to while I'm in here, or I'll sue this county for ever' penny it's got."

"You can make a phone call," Rhodes said. "Call somebody about your roosters."

Henry didn't say anything for at least a minute.

"The county will pay for the call if you don't have a quarter," Rhodes said.

"It ain't that," Henry said at last.

"Well, what is it then?"

"I ain't got nobody to call."

Rhodes had always known that he wasn't really hard-boiled enough to be a legendary lawman like, say, Dirty Harry Callahan. It was in situations like this one that he sometimes found himself feeling sorry for the malefactors.

"How about someone in Thurston?" he asked.

Henry was sitting on the bunk, his fingers laced together and his hands dangling between his legs. He didn't look up at Rhodes.

"I said I ain't got nobody."

So, since Rhodes was determined to hold Henry for at least twenty-four hours, that was how he found himself in charge of a flock of stags.

Ivy didn't seem enthusiastic about the idea of feeding and watering a bunch of roosters raised for fighting. Rhodes didn't especially blame her, but he tried not to let it show.

"It might be educational," he said. "You've probably never seen a flock of stags before."

"I thought stags were deer."

Rhodes explained how the term applied to roosters.

"Well," Ivy said, "you're right. I've never seen a flock of stags. And I'm not sure that I want to."

"It's a nice drive in the country," he said. "And we could eat at the Jolly Tamale."

"You've tried that one on me already this week. But why not? You've been pretty good lately. You deserve it."

Rhodes hadn't told her about the sandwich he'd had for lunch, and he hadn't mentioned his fight with Henry. He was walking all right, and she hadn't noticed anything wrong. He didn't think this would be a good time to say anything about either the fight or the sandwich.

"You're right," he said. "I deserve it."

He didn't say why.

It was on the drive to Thurston that Ivy brought up something that Rhodes hadn't thought about.

"You remember when we were talking to Press Yardley about the emus?" she asked.

It wasn't really a question, but Rhodes said that he did.

"He said that he went into Obert for some groceries the night his emus were stolen, didn't he?"

Rhodes remembered the remark. "I think so. Why?"

"Where can you buy groceries in Obert at night? As far as that goes, where can you buy groceries in Obert in the daytime?"

Obert was even smaller than Thurston, and there was no real grocery store there.

"There's that little service station on the far side of town," Rhodes said. "They sell bread and milk and things like that."

"How late do they stay open?"

"Probably until just a little while after dark," Rhodes said.

"So Press didn't go into Obert to buy groceries when his emus were stolen," Ivy said. "Did he?"

"I don't guess he did," Rhodes said.

"So where was he, then?"

Rhodes took his eyes off the highway for a second to look at his wife. He wondered why he hadn't thought of that.

"That's a good question," he said. "I guess I'll have to ask him."

Rhodes and Ivy had no trouble feeding Henry's stags. The feed was located in the tin barn. It was hot and dusty inside, and Rhodes would have preferred not to spend any time there, but he looked around until he saw a water bucket hanging on a nail.

He left the barn, went to the well, and filled the bucket while Ivy put feed out. The stags were well-behaved. It appeared that they were aggressive only with other trained fighters.

"Can you imagine what it must be like around here in the morning?" Ivy asked.

Rhodes had always liked the sound of a rooster crowing in the early morning, but he didn't think he'd like the sound of thirty or so of them crowing.

"Noisy," he said.

"What kind of roosters are these?" Ivy asked, putting out feed for a reddish-colored stag.

Rhodes didn't know enough about fighting roosters to distinguish one kind from another, though he did know the names of some of the different breeds.

"Some of them might be Commodore Grays, and there might be a few Valley Roundheads or Wyatt Hackle Cocks. Or there might not be."

Some of the roosters were definitely gray-colored, but that didn't mean that any of the names Rhodes had called was correct, and he admitted as much.

"What kind of chickens lay eggs?" Ivy asked.

Rhodes knew the answer to that one. "Hens lay eggs."

Ivy threw a handful of feed at him. "You know what I mean."

Rhodes knew. She meant the kind of hens that Henry had been talking about earlier, the kind that lived in cages. Rhodes wondered if it might be better to find someplace that sold eggs from free-range chickens. That is, if Ivy would ever let him eat another egg.

"Laying hens are usually white leghorns, I think," he said.

"And leghorn roosters don't fight?"

"Only Foghorn Leghorn," Rhodes said. "And he usually fights a dog."

"Who's Foghorn Leghorn?" Ivy asked.

"Never mind," Rhodes said.

It was getting dark when Rhodes and Ivy finished their meal at the Jolly Tamale and left the restaurant. Rhodes was feeling stuffed after eating a combination platter, which included a tamale, two enchiladas, beans, rice, tortillas, guacamole, chili con queso, and chips.

"Do you think Red Rogers would approve of your going to dinner in the county car?" Ivy asked.

"Probably not unless it was official business," Rhodes said. "Which it is."

Ivy poked him in the stomach with her index finger. "You call eating official business?"

"I didn't mean the meal," Rhodes told her. "We were tending to business at Wally Henry's place, and I have another stop to make. We just happened to take time out to eat between destinations."

Ivy nodded. "I see. And what's our next stop?"

"Mine," Rhodes said. "I'll take you home first."

"Why?"

"I don't think you need to visit the Palm Club."

"Why not?" Ivy wanted to know. "It might be fun."

"Or then again," Rhodes said, "it might not."

While he was at home, Rhodes fed his dog, Speedo, and gave him a short romp. Because of the heat, neither of them felt like romping for long, and Rhodes's ankle wasn't up to a great deal of strenuous activity. After a few minutes he went back into the house and called Dr. Slick.

"Emu feathers for sure." Slick said. "That camper was full of them."

"That's what I thought," Rhodes said.

"But you had to make certain, right?"

"That's right. Thanks for your help." Rhodes started to hang up, and then he had another thought. "You haven't treated any roosters lately, have you?"

He heard Slick's laugh at the other end of the line. "You mean for injuries sustained in the course of a cockfight?"

"Well, I was just wondering."

"Sheriff, the men who fight roosters don't bring them in to a vet for treatment. If the injuries aren't too serious, they treat them themselves with whatever kind of home remedy they've cooked up. And if the injuries are severe, they put the birds out of their misery. In my entire career, I've never treated a fighting cock."

"It was just a thought," Rhodes said.

"Believe me, I'd help you if I could," the vet said. "I don't like the idea of using birds for blood sport any more than you do."

Rhodes thanked him and hung up. At least he knew that Lige Ward had been hauling emus around in the back of his truck.

The Palm Club was on the outskirts of Clearview on the road to Milsby, a tiny community that was barely hanging on to its existence. Milsby was the home of Mrs. Wilkie, who had once set her cap for Rhodes, without success.

The Palm Club had been a Clearview fixture since most people could remember, though Rhodes couldn't see what its appeal was. Its only claim to fame was that once, in the latter part of the 1960s, Jerry Lee Lewis, having lost his huge rock-and-roll following and attempting to make a comeback in the country field, had played a couple of sets there one night.

The ill-lighted parking lot of the club was covered with crushed white gravel, and there were pickups and cars parked all over it, with no attempt at being orderly. Country music came from two speakers located under the overhang of the roof near the entrance.

Rhodes parked on the edge of the lot and got out of his car just as Garth Brooks finished singing about his friends in low places. There was only a brief pause before Brooks and Dunn started in on "Boot Scootin' Boogie."

Rhodes wound his way through the cars toward the door. The Palm Club was a low square building with no windows and no distinguishing features. Rhodes had no idea why it was called the Palm Club. There was nothing tropical or exotic about it, just a fading sign over the entrance with the words PALM CLUB, flanked by two drooping trees with what looked like either coconuts or bowling balls almost hidden among the leaves.

When Rhodes opened the door, the music increased in volume so suddenly that he blinked. The lighting wasn't much better inside than it was outside, and a lot of it came from the various red-and-blue neon signs advertising beer. Rhodes could see a great many couples boot-scootin' on the big square of hardwood that made up the middle of the club.

There were also a lot of people sitting at tables, talking, Rhodes supposed. Their mouths were moving, but he didn't see how they could hear one another. Nearly all the men and quite a few of the women were wearing jeans, western shirts, and big white or black cowboy hats, though some of the women were wearing full skirts that flounced while they danced.

There was a long wooden bar running down the side of

the club opposite the door, and the mirror behind it reflected the dancers and the few singles sitting on the barstools. The Palm Club didn't have a no-smoking policy, and a grayish cloud hovered near the low ceiling.

No one paid much attention to Rhodes as he twisted his way through the maze of tables around the edge of the dance floor. They'd seen lawmen in the Palm Club often enough when one of the occasional fights got out of hand.

"Boot Scootin' Boogie" ended. "Achy Breaky Heart" came on, and more couples joined the dancing. Rhodes felt very old. Not only could he remember Charlie Pride, he could remember Hank Williams, Sr. Probably he was the only one in the club who could. For that matter, he was probably one of only a few who knew who Willie Nelson or Waylon Jennings was.

When Rhodes got to the bar he saw that Burl Griffin was behind it. Griffin owned a small share of the club and was the regular bartender; he had dealt with Rhodes before. He was dressed exactly like the customers, except that he had on a sparkling white apron. He nodded to Rhodes and came over to where Rhodes was standing, well away from the nearest customer.

"We haven't had any fights in here tonight that I know of, Sheriff," Griffin said, leaning across the bar so he could be heard over the music. "If you got a call, it was just some kid calling in for a joke."

"What about last night?" Rhodes asked. "Have any fights then?"

"Coupla guys got into an argument over whose turn it was to buy a pretty lady in tight-fittin' jeans a longneck. Didn't amount to much. One guy knocked the other one down and went off with the lady. She seemed pretty satisfied that he was the winner. That was about it."

Rhodes nodded and then brought up the night he was really interested in. "And night before last? Were you on duty then?"

"Yeah, I was here." Griffin thought for a minute. "I see what you're getting at."

"What's that?" Rhodes asked.

Griffin leaned closer. "Lige Ward was in here night before last."

"I thought he might've been. Who else was here?"

Griffin straightened up and looked around the room, taking in the size of the crowd. "Are you kidding me, Sheriff?"

"You know what I mean," Rhodes said.

Griffin leaned down. "I guess I do at that."

"So?" Rhodes said.

"So, yeah, Lige got into a little scuffle."

"And you just happened not to get around to letting me know."

"Hey, it was nothing," Griffin protested. "You know the Palm Club likes to cooperate with the law. We run a family-type business here."

Rhodes hadn't noticed any families. "When a man gets killed, it's not nothing."

"I didn't mean about Lige getting killed. I was sorry to hear that. I mean the fight, if you want to call it that. It was nothing. You know I've called you more than once about Lige when things got out of hand."

That was true, but Griffin's definition of things getting out of hand didn't necessarily agree with Rhodes's. With Griffin, getting out of hand meant a near riot.

"Tell me about the little scuffle," Rhodes said.

"It was like the one last night," Griffin said. "There wasn't much to it."

Rhodes wasn't anywhere near satisfied by that explanation. "Be more specific," he said.

"Hey, Lige didn't even start it," Griffin said. "Somebody else did. Lige just jumped into the middle of it. I guess you could say he was the one that stopped it."

"Who was involved?"

"Bunch of kids," Griffin said. He hesitated. "And one other guy."

"Who?"

"You might know him," Griffin said. "Comes in here every now and then. Name's Wally Henry."

11

▼

BEFORE HE WENT HOME AFTER HIS VISIT TO THE PALM CLUB, Rhodes made the short drive out to Obert. The little service station that sold bread and milk was closed. Rhodes got out of the car and checked the hand-printed sign inside the glass door.

SUMMER HOURS
OPEN 6:30 A.M.
CLOSE 8:30 P.M.

That pretty well meant that Press Yardley hadn't been getting any groceries after dark in Obert. So where had he been?

Rhodes thought about going by Yardley's house to ask, but it was getting late, Rhodes's ankle hurt, his ribs hurt, and for that matter, he pretty much hurt all over. He decided to wait until the next day. He got back in the car and drove home, thinking about Lige Ward and Wally Henry.

The way Burl Griffin had described the fight, Wally had been arguing with three young men, probably about who was supposed to be sitting at what table. Lige was sitting by himself at a table nearby, not paying much attention until

Henry lunged across the table at the men, trying to brain one of them with a beer bottle.

"Lige was just sitting there most of the night," Griffin said. "Sunk in the blues like he is most of the time. But the fight got him interested. I was glad to see it, to tell you the truth. I don't like to see a fella sitting there broodin' all evening. That's the kind that can cause you real trouble."

Rhodes knew what Griffin was getting at. "Real trouble" to the bartender meant guns or knives. Or both. There had been real trouble at the Palm Club more than once.

"So Lige pulled Henry off," Rhodes said. "Then what?"

"They scuffled around a little, but that was all. Nobody got hurt."

"What did Lige do after that?"

Griffin considered the question. He had obviously lost interest in the fight as soon as it was over.

"I think they left together," he said finally.

"Who?" Rhodes asked.

"Lige and Wally. They went out together. I thought they might've been going to finish the fight outside in the parking lot, but they didn't. They were looking pretty friendly."

"What about the others?"

Griffin didn't remember. "They must've gone right on drinking beer. Otherwise I'd have noticed them."

"Did Lige and Henry come back?"

"Hey, you're right. I didn't think of that. Wally didn't, but Lige did. He came back after about a half hour and sat down with those fellas that Wally jumped on."

"What happened then?" Rhodes asked.

"Nothing that I remember. I guess the fellas thanked Lige for what he did. Maybe they bought him a few beers. Who knows? They didn't cause any more trouble."

"What did they look like?"

Griffin waved a hand at the dancers and the table-sitters. Everyone in the Palm Club was dressed pretty much the same: cowboy hats, boots, western shirts, jeans.

"Take your pick," Griffin said.

It was no help at all, but it was the best Griffin could do. Rhodes would have given a lot to know who the three men were. It was possible they'd been the last ones to see Lige alive. He would also have liked to know what Lige and Henry had talked about in the parking lot. He'd have to ask Henry about that tomorrow, before he talked to Press Yardley again. And he had to see Nard King about that bill of sale for the emus. Might as well keep questioning him. Maybe he'd cave in and admit that Lige had stolen them for him.

But Rhodes didn't really think so.

Because of all the strenuous exercise, or maybe because of the heavy meal, Rhodes overslept the next morning. Ivy had left him a note, reminding him to eat his shredded wheat, which he did in penance for having eaten at the Jolly Tamale the night before. He gave Speedo some Old Roy dog food and some water before leaving for the jail.

Ruth Grady was waiting when he got there. She had come up with what Rhodes considered the final proof that Lige Ward had stolen Yardley's emus.

"There's not any doubt about it?" he asked.

"Not a bit," Ruth said. "This cast is a perfect match for the shoes Clyde Ballinger gave me. See this notch in the heel?"

She pointed to what appeared to be a V-shaped cut.

"I see it," Rhodes said.

"With something like that, it's almost impossible to make a mistake. Lige Ward was at those pens. I can't prove he took anything out of them, but he was there."

"That's good enough for now," Rhodes told her. "What about that GMC truck of Wally Henry's?" Did anybody around Obert see it out there the morning Mrs. Ward was killed?"

"I haven't found anybody yet who did," she said. "I'll keep looking."

"Don't spend too much time on it. Keep as much as you can to your regular patrol. But ask whenever you get the chance."

Ruth said that she would and left. Rhodes went upstairs to have a little chat with Wally Henry.

Henry was in a pretty good mood, having been fed the jail's regular breakfast of sausage, eggs, and toast. But he still wasn't doing any talking about the cockfight. In fact, he still wasn't admitting that he'd been there.

"I don't know what you're talkin' about, Sheriff," he said. "I told you yesterday that I just raise roosters, and that's all I do. I don't have a thing to do with fightin' 'em."

"Maybe so," Rhodes said. "But you were seen talking to Lige Ward at the Palm Club after the fight. Seems like the two of you were downright buddy-buddy."

Henry, who was sitting on the bunk, leaned back against the wall.

"I don't know who told you a thing like that, but they must've mistook somebody else for me."

Rhodes looked at Henry's pigtail and wondered how the man could think anyone could make a mistaken identification of him.

"There wasn't any mistake," Rhodes said. "It was you, all right. You were about to swat somebody with a beer bottle before Lige pulled you off."

Henry crossed his thick arms in front of his chest and narrowed his small eyes.

"I don't recall anything like that," he said, but he was plainly lying. "Just never happened."

"After that, you and Lige went out into the parking lot," Rhodes said. "I'd like to know what you talked about."

"Never happened," Henry insisted. "Whoever told you that story's got me mixed up with somebody else, that's all."

"I was told by an eyewitness."

"Who?"

"Never mind who. He saw you and Lige. You might as well tell me about it."

"Can't tell you what didn't happen." Henry uncrossed his arms and leaned forward on the bunk. "Tell you one thing, though. You bring this witness in here and let him look at me. Then we'll see if he tells the same story."

Rhodes didn't think Burl Griffin would be afraid of Henry, but he was also pretty sure that Griffin wouldn't want to testify against any of his customers. Rhodes was going to have to break Henry down some other way. Maybe he could locate one or two of the men Henry had jumped. They would be a lot more willing to testify against him than Griffin.

"I'll think about it," Rhodes said. "You might do some thinking, too."

"I won't have to think long. I'll be bonded out of here pretty quick." Henry paused. "You take care of my stags last evenin'?"

Rhodes told him what he'd done.

"I 'preciate that," Henry said.

"I'm going to find out about you and Lige," Rhodes said.

Henry smiled. "Sure you are," he said.

When Rhodes got back to the office, Hack was practically bouncing up and down in his chair. Rhodes didn't know why, but he knew that the dispatcher had something he wanted to say. He wondered how long it would take him to get Hack to say it. He went on over to his desk.

"What about it, Hack?" he said, indicating the cast that Ruth had left there. "Pretty good police work, right?"

"It ain't bad," Hack acknowledged, which was about all the praise Rhodes had expected. Hack hadn't liked the idea of a woman deputy at first, though he had come to appreciate Ruth nearly as much as Rhodes did.

"I can tell you somethin' better, though."

"What's that?"

Hack patted the computer monitor. "You remember how long I had to tell you we needed this before you finally gave in and got it?"

"I remember." Rhodes hoped they weren't going to get into that old discussion again.

"Well, you just never know how much you might need a thing until you get it. It can pay off in a big way sometimes."

Rhodes wondered what Hack was getting at, but there was nothing he could do except play along.

"You're right about that," he said. "You even got rid of Red Rogers with it."

Hack smiled. "That ain't all I got."

"Okay," Rhodes said. "Tell me what else."

"You remember you told me to get in touch with the fella in Wichita Falls that owned the murder gun?"

Rhodes remembered, but he hadn't thought much about it. He didn't think it would lead to anything.

"Well, I called him," Hack said. "Didn't get him, though."

Rhodes didn't see what good the call had done if Hack hadn't talked to anyone.

"Got his answering machine," Hack explained. "Told it why I was callin' and told it I wanted the fella to call me back."

"And did he call?"

"Just a little while before you come back from the cells."

Rhodes waited, thinking that Hack might go on. He should have known better. Hack always had to be asked.

"What did he have to say?"

Hack settled back in his chair, always a bad sign. "Turns out that he's a law-abidin' citizen. The gun wasn't stolen or anything. Turns out he sold it on the up-and-up."

Just as Rhodes had suspected, not that it made any difference. The pistol had probably traveled through flea markets all over the state before winding up in Blacklin County.

"I guess that's the end of it, then," he said.

"No, it ain't," Hack said.

Rhodes waited. Hack sat there in silence.

"Why not?" Rhodes asked finally.

"He kept a record of who he sold it to."

Now that was a first. Rhodes could never remember anything like that happening before.

"Who was it?" Rhodes asked, knowing that if the answer was Wally Henry, the case was the next thing to closed.

"It was a legitimate gun dealer," Hack said. "Up in Dallas. Seems like this fella in Wichita Falls buys and sells guns all the time, but he mostly deals in .357s and .44s, which is why he remembered that little .38. He had the serial number and all, though, so it's not just his memory we're goin' on here."

Rhodes was glad to hear that, he supposed, but he didn't know what good it did them to know that a dealer in Dallas had bought the pistol. He said as much to Hack.

"What good it does us is that the dealer sold it to somebody else," Hack explained.

Now they were finally going to get to it, Rhodes thought. "Who bought it from him?"

"You ain't gonna believe this," Hack said, drawing it out as long as he could.

"Try me," Rhodes said.

"Press Yardley," Hack told him.

Hack's news about the pistol had set Rhodes back for a minute. It seemed that his theories about Wally Henry might not be correct after all.

It was easy enough to create a narrative in which Press Yardley was the villain. He could have come back home from buying groceries, or wherever he had been, as Lige was driving away with the emus, followed Lige to Nard King's place, and shot him. Yardley didn't look big enough to have put Lige in the portable toilet, but Rhodes couldn't rule out the possibility. Yardley could have dropped the pistol at the toilet, and Michael Ferrin and his buddies could have found it. Somehow Rayjean Ward might have found out about what Yardley had done, confronted him, and gotten killed herself.

Of course there were quite a few questions left unanswered by that theory.

Why did Press let Lige unload the emus in King's pen?

Why was he at the cockpit when he killed Rayjean?

And if he hadn't been buying groceries, where had he been?

And why had he lied about it?

All of which made it more important than ever to get the ballistics report back from the lab. Rhodes had to know whether the .38 he'd taken from Michael Ferrin had fired the shots that killed Lige Ward.

Rhodes thought it was time to go and have a talk with Press Yardley, even though he didn't have the report yet. He was almost out the door when the phone rang.

"It's for you," Hack called. "Miz Appleby."

Rhodes walked back over to the phone. "Hello, Mrs. Appleby," he said. "What can we do for you today?"

"It's Claude and Clyde," she said. "They've got something to tell you."

"All right," Rhodes said.

"They're not here," Mrs. Appleby said. "Are you going by Wal-Mart's anytime today?"

"I could do that," Rhodes said, wondering why.

"They both got summer jobs there yesterday," Mrs. Appleby told him. "Stock boys."

"That's good," Rhodes said. This was turning out to be like a conversation with Hack.

"Anyway, what they have to tell you has to do with Wal-Mart's," she said. "They didn't want to talk to me about it."

That explained a lot. "I'll go by there in a few minutes and talk to them," Rhodes said.

"I hope it's important," Mrs. Appleby said. "I don't like to have them bothering you for nothing."

"I'm sure it's important," Rhodes said. "I'm glad to do it."

"Thank you, Sheriff. They really are good boys, you know."

"I'm sure they are," Rhodes told her, though he wasn't. "I'm glad they've got jobs."

"I am, too. They're working in the back, in the warehouse area."

"I'll stop by and see them," Rhodes promised.

Rhodes pulled up near the loading dock in the back of the Wal-Mart store and stopped the car. By the time he was out the door, Clyde (or Claude) was heading toward him. Rhodes was pretty sure it was Clyde.

"I been watchin' for you," Clyde said. "Let's us go over there." He pointed to a stack of empty cardboard boxes that had held TV sets.

Rhodes followed him over to the stack. Clyde kept on going and went behind the boxes before he stopped.

"I didn't want anybody to see me talking to you," he explained when Rhodes joined him. "Don't want to get in bad on the job the first day."

"That's all right," Rhodes said. He was used to that attitude. "What did you want to tell me?"

"It's about that cockfight," Clyde said. "The one me and Claude said we didn't go to."

Rhodes was gratified to see that he had identified the right twin.

"What about the cockfight?" he asked.

Clyde looked over the top of the boxes, then back at Rhodes. "We didn't exactly tell the truth about that."

For some reason that bit of news didn't come as much of a shock to Rhodes.

"So you did go," he said.

Clyde shook his head. "Not exactly. We weren't invited, and we don't like to push in where we're not wanted."

Rhodes thought that Clyde wasn't telling the whole truth again. Both Clyde and Claude had a way of turning up in a lot of places where they weren't supposed to be and where no one had invited them.

"How can you 'not exactly' go to a cockfight?" Rhodes asked.

"It was like we sort of watched it from the trees," Clyde said. "We couldn't see much."

"You must have seen something. Otherwise you wouldn't have wanted to talk to me."

"Yeah. But we didn't know what we seen until yesterday."

Rhodes thought for a second that maybe it was his fault. Maybe everyone was somehow making perfect sense and he just wasn't catching on. But it did seem that more and more of his conversations were composed mostly of non sequiturs.

"Yesterday was a long time after the fight," he pointed out.

"Sure," Clyde agreed. "I know that."

"So why didn't you find out what you'd seen until then?"

"We had to get the job here first."

That didn't make any more sense than anything else Clyde had told him.

"What does this job have to do with the cockfight?"

"Nothing," Clyde said.

At least Rhodes was well trained in this kind of discussion, so he had no difficulty in holding up his end of it.

"Then why did you want to talk to me?"

"Well, it's about who we saw at that cockfight. Except we didn't know we saw him until yesterday."

"I see," Rhodes said, though he didn't see at all.

"What it is," Clyde said, "is that we saw this guy there, but we didn't know who he was till we got this job."

"Oh," Rhodes said.

"We'd never seen him before," Clyde said. "To us, he was just another guy at the cockfight. But then we saw him again yesterday. He talked to us before he hired us."

"Who is he?" Rhodes asked. He had a premonition that he wasn't going to like the answer.

"It was Mr. Keene," Clyde said. "He's the manager of the store here."

Rhodes had been right. He didn't like the answer, but now the conversation made a lot more sense. He had another question for Clyde, however.

"There was someone else there I'd like to ask you about," he said.

"Ever'body was wearing caps and hats," Clyde said. "We couldn't see too many faces."

"You don't need to have seen his face," Rhodes told him. "Just his hair. He wears it in a long pigtail, nearly to his waist."

"Oh, yeah," Clyde said. "Yeah. We saw a guy like that."

"You're sure?" he asked.

"Big guy?" Clyde said. "Has a beard? He was there, all right. Looked like he had a rooster in the fight."

There probably weren't two men in Blacklin County who fit that description. Henry had been at the fight, all right, and he had lied about it. Rhodes wasn't surprised.

Clyde went back into the warehouse. Rhodes stayed outside to think for a minute. Wally Henry was still his strongest suspect in the Wards's murders, but Press Yardley seemed to be tied up in things somehow. And now it looked as if Hal Keene might have a stronger motive for murder than the simple fact that Lige Ward had chained himself to the front doors of Wal-Mart a couple of times.

Lige might have indulged in a little blackmail on the side. He might have threatened to expose Keene as someone who took part in illegal activities. Rhodes knew that Keene was a member of a number of civic organizations that wouldn't like it if one of their members got unfavorable publicity by being arrested for betting on cockfights. And Rhodes suspected that the Wal-Mart hierarchy might not take kindly to having one of their store managers mixed up in gambling and cockfighting. It wasn't the kind of thing that looked good on a résumé.

Lige couldn't have exposed Keene's part in those things without exposing his own, however, and Rhodes didn't think that any kind of threat would be enough to drive Keene to murder. Nevertheless, because of the connections between the two men, Rhodes thought he'd better have a talk with Keene.

He stepped from behind the boxes and walked into the warehouse area. He saw Claude pushing a dolly loaded with exercise equipment still in the boxes. Clyde was getting another stack ready to be moved, and there was a gangly teenager stacking some large but obviously not heavy cardboard boxes whose contents weren't labeled. No one else was working in the warehouse.

There were a few salesclerks and register operators on their break in another part of the huge room, gathered at some tables near soft-drink machines that offered Sam's Cola. There was a candy machine, too, along with a coffeemaker on a table littered with disposable cups, plastic spoons, and packets of sweeteners and creamer.

Keene's office was set off from the rest of the room, well away from the break area. There was a large window in the side wall so that Keene could see and be seen, so Rhodes knew the manager was in his office, sitting at the desk.

Rhodes knocked on the door, and Keene said, "Come in."

Rhodes went inside and closed the door behind him. "Good morning, Mr. Keene," he said.

"Good morning, Sheriff. I saw you out there in the warehouse. Is there something wrong? I hope nobody's chained to the doors again."

"Not that I know of," Rhodes said. "But I would like to talk to you for a minute about Lige Ward."

Keene indicated a plastic lawn chair near the desk. "It's not fancy, but it's comfortable. Have a seat."

Rhodes sat. The chair didn't seem to him to be as comfortable as advertised.

"Now, what about Lige?" Keene asked. "I'm sorry to hear he got himself killed, but I'm not really surprised. He was a little loony, if you ask me."

"We all have our little quirks," Rhodes said, shifting in the plastic chair. It scraped on the floor beneath him.

Keene chuckled. "I guess we do at that."

"Some of us like cockfighting, for instance," Rhodes said.

Keene stopped chuckling.

"You must have known it would come out sooner or later that you were there," Rhodes said. "More than one person saw you."

"Who else have they told?" Keene asked.

"Nobody, as far as I know. Why?"

"Because I can't have it getting out that I was there. Don't you see, Sheriff? I'm a respected member of the community. I can't have people knowing I was at a cockfight."

Rhodes thought that it was a little late for Keene to start worrying about that now. And he wondered if he hadn't been wrong. Maybe Keene *would* kill to keep people from finding out about his participation.

"Why did you go then?" he asked.

Keene got up and walked around his desk. He looked out the window as if afraid someone in the warehouse might overhear him. Rhodes looked out, too. There was no one nearby, and no one seemed interested in the office.

"I don't know why I went," Keene said. "Curiosity, I

guess. I didn't even know that Lige Ward was involved until I got there. Somebody who comes to the store here a lot happened to mention the fight to me. I'd always heard about things like that, but I'd never seen anything like it except in the movies, so I thought I might go, just to see what it was all about." He shook his head. "It was a mistake."

"Because someone saw you?"

"Because it was terrible. It wasn't exciting. It was just bloody." Keene's face seemed to pale a little at the thought. "I had to leave before anyone else. I couldn't take it."

"Didn't you think that someone might see you there?" Rhodes asked.

"I thought that if they did, they wouldn't say anything. After all, they were doing the same thing I was."

"But you didn't know that Lige would be there. He might have decided to say something, since he's not one of your biggest fans. Why didn't you leave as soon as you saw him?"

"I don't think he even recognized me," Keene said. "I stood back from the rest, didn't talk to anyone. I didn't think *anyone* recognized me."

"What about the person who mentioned it to you?"

"He wasn't even there," Keene said. "His name's Gad Pullens. He sits in the lobby and watches the customers come and go. I talk to him now and then."

"And you're sure Lige didn't see you?"

"I'm sure. He never even looked my way." Keene had been looking down, but now his head snapped up. "Surely you don't think I had anything to do with killing him. I swear to you, Sheriff—"

"You sell pistols here?" Rhodes asked.

"Yes, we do, but—"

"Do you own a pistol?"

"No. No. My wife would never allow one in the house, not even for self-protection. She thinks they're dangerous."

Keene paused, looking out the window again. "She doesn't like hunting, either. She thinks it's cruel to animals. She doesn't have to know I went to the cockfight, does she, Sheriff?"

"We'll see," Rhodes said. "Sometimes these things have a way of getting out."

"But I didn't kill Lige Ward! I didn't even stay till the end of the first cockfight that day. I walked back to my car and left."

"You have access to handguns, you and Ward didn't get along, and you were seen not too far from where he was killed," Rhodes pointed out.

"That doesn't prove anything!"

Rhodes admitted that it didn't. "Did you see Lige after the fight?"

"He didn't make it a habit to visit the store," Keene said.

"I don't mean as a customer. Did he come by and talk to you, say anything about the fight?"

"What do you mean? I told you he didn't see me. Why would he say anything about the fight to me?"

"I was just wondering," Rhodes said.

"Look, Sheriff. I didn't kill anybody, and I didn't see Lige Ward again after the fight. I was at home with my wife the night he was killed. We watched TV and then went to bed. I didn't leave the house."

"Will your wife verify that?"

"Of course she will, if she has to. But I hope you won't have to ask her. Can't you just take my word for it?"

Rhodes didn't laugh. He said, "It's not that I don't trust you. It's just that I don't make a habit of taking people's word for something when a crime is involved, especially a crime like murder."

"I guess I can understand that. But I didn't do anything, Sheriff."

"I don't think you did," Rhodes said. "It's just that I don't like coincidences."

Keene went back to his chair and sat down. He moved a few papers around on his desk and then looked at Rhodes.

"I wish I'd never gone to that cockfight," he said.

"I don't much blame you," Rhodes said.

12

▼

LEAVING WAL-MART, RHODES WAS CONVINCED THAT KEENE was telling the truth, just as he had been convinced that Wally Henry was lying.

The trouble was, as Rhodes had told Keene, the sheriff didn't like coincidences, and this case was full of them. First Brother Alton had turned up at the scene of Rayjean Ward's murder, and now he had learned that Keene had been at the cockfight. Brother Alton had been at the creek when Lige's body was found, and Keene had been on the outs with the Wards. And while Rhodes didn't think either of the men was a murderer, there was a nagging little doubt at the back of his mind, a little voice saying something like, "You never can tell."

When Rhodes came out from behind the building, he saw that the parking·lot was again filled with cars. Both the discount house and the supermarket were doing a land-office business. If he were to drive through downtown Clearview, he thought, there wouldn't be five cars parked on the street. He decided not to go that way.

Rhodes drove between the two wooden Indians, neither of which had improved in appearance since his last visit, and onto Press Yardley's property. As he got out of the car, he saw Yardley in the emu pens. Yardley's dog was sniffing around the outside of the fence, but he looked up when he heard the car and came running over as soon as Rhodes got out.

The dog jumped up on Rhodes, who rubbed his head before shoving him aside and walking over to the pens. The dog, not at all offended by Rhodes's cavalier treatment, followed the sheriff, running beside him, in front of him, and once getting between his legs and nearly tripping him up. He never stopped barking.

The emus paid the dog's yapping no more attention than they had the first time Rhodes had visited. Rhodes still thought it was strange to see such odd birds in the middle of Texas. Wally Henry's roosters were a lot more familiar.

Yardley met Rhodes at the fence. He didn't look especially happy to see who his visitor was.

"Good morning, Sheriff," Yardley said, not sounding as if he meant it. "Found out anything about my missing emus yet?"

"Maybe," Rhodes said. "I'm not absolutely sure. I've found something else, too."

"What's that?"

"Your pistol," Rhodes said.

Yardley's face fell even further.

"You want to tell me about it?" Rhodes asked.

Yardley didn't appear to have anything to say. He stood in his pen, watching one of the emus scratching in the dirt. The dog stopped barking and resumed its sniffing along the fence line. Rhodes watched the dog for a second, then looked at Yardley.

"Did you shoot Lige?" Rhodes asked.

"No," Yardley said, after what Rhodes thought was too long a pause. "I didn't. I tried to, but I didn't."

"What happened?" Rhodes asked. "Did you catch him stealing the emus and take a shot at him?"

"No. Of course not. I'd never have called you here if that had been the case. I'm not even sure he's the one who took them."

"Why did you shoot him, then?"

"I *didn't* shoot him. I said I tried to. There's a difference."

"All right," Rhodes said. "Why did you try to?"

"It's a long story," Yardley said. "Let's go in the house, and I'll tell you about it."

Yardley had half a pot of coffee sitting on the coffeemaker in the kitchen. He pulled the carafe off the machine and held it up.

"Want a cup?" he asked Rhodes.

Rhodes, who preferred to get his caffeine from Dr Pepper, declined.

"I think I'll pour one for myself," Yardley said. "Have a seat at the table, Sheriff."

Rhodes sat at the round oak table while Yardley got a thin china cup and saucer out of the kitchen cabinet. The table was at the end of the kitchen beside a sliding glass door. Rhodes looked through the door; he could see the emus walking around in the pen. The dog was nowhere in sight.

The cup and saucer clinked when Yardley put them on the table. Then he sat in the chair opposite Rhodes. He took a sip of the coffee.

"Obviously Lige and I had our differences, Sheriff," Yardley said, putting the cup down. "But I didn't kill him."

"Tell me about your differences."

"Well, you know about the guineas."

"They made noise," Rhodes said. "They bothered you."

"They *are* noisy," Yardley said.

Rhodes agreed. He'd heard them himself only recently.

"Anyway," Yardley went on, "it all started with the guineas."

"*What* started with the guineas?"

"Me and Ray——" There was a catch in Yardley's voice, and he had to stop for a second. He took another sip of coffee. "Me and Rayjean," he finished.

"What about you and Rayjean?" Rhodes asked, wondering if Ivy could have been right.

"We were . . . having an affair."

Well, well, Rhodes thought. Ivy *had* been right. Rhodes remembered the Victoria's Secret catalog. He'd thought that Rayjean Ward had been trying to find a little lacy something to help hold her marriage to Lige together, and he'd felt sorry for her. But maybe it hadn't been that at all. Instead, maybe she'd been thinking about finding some new ways to please Press Yardley.

Yardley went on with his story. "Before I ever called you about the guineas, I went over to Lige's place to talk to him about them, to see if we could work something out. He wasn't there, so I talked to Rayjean. We seemed to hit it off, but nothing came of it."

"Something must have," Rhodes said.

"That was later. The guineas kept on making noise, and they were roosting in the woods closer and closer to my house, so I finally called you. After you talked to him, Lige came over and threatened me. I told him to leave me alone. He just laughed, and then I told him I had a gun."

Yardley stopped talking and drank some more coffee.

"That's it?" Rhodes said. "I thought you tried to shoot him."

"That was later, too. Rayjean came over here the next day to apologize, and we hit it off again. She was having a hard time with Lige. He was going out and drinking and getting into fights. She needed someone to talk to."

"She must have needed more than that," Rhodes said.

"There's no need to be crude, Sheriff. It wasn't the way you think."

Rhodes resisted the urge to ask exactly how it was. He didn't want to be accused of being crude again. Besides, he figured it *was* pretty much the way he thought it was. There weren't too many possible variations on the theme.

"That's where you were the night Lige was killed," Rhodes said. "With Rayjean. You didn't go into Obert for groceries, because you can't buy groceries in Obert at night."

Yardley smiled ruefully. "I thought of that after I told you. I wasn't sure you caught it."

Rhodes didn't see any need to tell him that Ivy had been the one to catch it.

"Lige was gone off again, 'honky-tonking,' Rayjean called it. So she phoned me and I went over for a while."

"It doesn't look very good for you," Rhodes said. "Your pistol has turned up, and it's the same caliber as the gun that killed Lige. Now Rayjean is dead, within walking distance from your house. You admit you were with her on the night Lige was killed. And you say you tried to shoot Lige."

"I guess it looks pretty bad, all right. I wouldn't shoot anyone, though. You must know that, Sheriff."

Rhodes wasn't sure what he knew anymore. "Tell me about shooting Lige."

"*Trying* to shoot him. I missed."

"Tell me about missing him, then."

"He found out about me and Rayjean," Yardley said. "He came over here one day and banged on the door. I thought he was going to break it down. He was yelling and banging and making threats, so I got the pistol out of the closet before I went to the door."

"When was that?" Rhodes asked.

"The day before he got shot."

"I see," Rhodes said.

Yardley shoved the cup and saucer aside. "That makes it look even worse for me, doesn't it. But you haven't heard the whole story yet."

"All right. Tell me."

"Well, I took the pistol to the door and opened it. Lige

came bustin' in and shoved me to the floor. He didn't give me a chance to say a word, just put his hand on my chest and shoved. That's when I tried to shoot him."

"But you missed," Rhodes said. "Is that right?"

"I didn't even pull the trigger. I was ashamed. I'd been fooling around with the man's wife. He had a right to push me around. I raised up the gun and pointed it at him, but I couldn't pull the trigger. I just said I was sorry and put the gun on the floor."

"What did Lige do then?"

"I thought he was going to beat me to a pulp, but he didn't. He yelled a lot and stormed around the room and called me a lot of names, and then he picked up the pistol. He told me that if I ever came near his wife again, he'd shoot me with my own gun. I believed him."

Rhodes thought about the bruise on Lige's chest.

"He shoved you. But you didn't shove back? You didn't hit him at all? Say, in the chest?"

"I didn't even move," Yardley said. "I just sat there. You should've heard him. I was too scared to fight." He thought about what Rhodes had said. "Why? Had he been in a fight?"

"He looked like it," Rhodes said.

"Probably the emus," Yardley told him.

"The emus?"

"They can kick like a mule. Well, they can kick, but not really that hard. An ostrich can, though. An ostrich can kick hard enough to kill you if he catches you right. But an emu can kick you pretty good if it tries. If you were trying to stuff one in the back seat of a car, it might thump you a good one."

Or in the back of a truck, Rhodes thought. Maybe that *was* how Lige had gotten bruised.

"So Lige took your pistol and left," he said.

"That's exactly right. I never saw him again after that."

Yardley looked out through the glass door as if Lige might be standing out in the backyard.

"But you saw Rayjean again," Rhodes said. "You must not have been scared for long."

"I only saw her," Yardley said, still looking out into the yard. "We didn't do anything. I told her that Lige knew about us and that I couldn't see her again."

"How did she take the news?"

Yardley turned to look at Rhodes. "She didn't like it any better than I did, but we knew Lige was right. We planned never to meet again after that night."

Rhodes almost believed him.

"That was the last time I saw her," Yardley said.

He got up, put the coffee cup and the saucer in the sink, and ran water in the cup. Then he sat back down.

"There's one thing I'd like to know," he said.

"Just one?" Rhodes said.

"For now. Can you tell me?"

"That depends on what it is."

"Where did you find the pistol? Did Lige have it?"

"No," Rhodes said. "It was someone else."

"Nard King," Yardley said. "He probably took it away from Lige and killed him with it."

"I didn't say that Lige was killed with your pistol," Rhodes reminded him.

Yardley looked surprised. "You sure implied it."

Rhodes couldn't help what people thought he was implying. He was more interested in the possibility that Yardley was right about Nard King.

"Why do you think King would shoot Lige?"

"It's obvious, isn't it?" Yardley said.

"Not to me," Rhodes told him. "Unless you're assuming that thieves fall out. That doesn't happen as often as you might think."

"Maybe King didn't want to pay for the emus once he

had them," Yardley suggested. "Or maybe Lige tried to hold him up for more money."

Rhodes didn't say so, but Yardley's ideas were at least as likely as most of the things Rhodes had come up with so far. The difference was that Yardley might just be trying to save his own neck by offering up some plausible theories that put the blame on someone else.

"There's one problem with those ideas," Rhodes said.

"What?"

"Nard King didn't have the gun," Rhodes said.

When Rhodes was through talking to Yardley, he went back outside to his car. He was almost there before the dog bounded up and tried to jump on him again. Rhodes took the time to pat the dog before getting in the car and calling Hack on the radio. He wanted to find out whether the ballistics report had come in.

"Nope," Hack said.

"Well, let me know if it does," Rhodes said, disappointed.

"We don't need it," Hack said. "Not right now, anyway."

Here we go again, Rhodes thought. "Why not?" he asked.

" 'Cause I called the lab," Hack said. "That's why."

"And what did they say?" Rhodes asked, relieved to get a straight answer for once.

"You sure you want me to tell you?" Hack asked. "Ever' scanner in the county's tuned in to us right now."

"Just give me a yes or no," Rhodes said, wondering if it was possible for Hack to do something that simple.

He hemmed and hawed for a few seconds, but finally he did it. "All right, then. The answer is yes."

Rhodes signed off. The slugs that had killed Lige Ward had come from Press Yardley's pistol.

* * *

Rhodes didn't go directly to Nard King's. Instead he drove down to the Ward place. As the guineas scattered in front of his car near the house, alerting the neighborhood, he thought about Rayjean and Press Yardley. You just never knew what might be going on behind closed doors.

Rhodes drove on down to the cockpit and got out of the car. There wasn't much of a breeze; the trees were nearly still, and while it was cooler in the shade of the trees than it had been in Yardley's emu pen, Rhodes could feel the heat filtering through the almost motionless leaves, along with an occasional ray of sun.

Lige's pickup was still parked where it had been, and for the first time Rhodes wondered what it was doing there. Why wasn't it at the house? Had someone killed Lige elsewhere and driven the truck here, or had Lige been killed right around this very spot?

Rhodes walked around the truck in widening circles, trying to find something that would give him a hint about what had happened on the night of Lige's death. He had searched the area earlier, but he hadn't had much of an idea of what he was looking for. Now he did.

After about five minutes, he found it.

There was a rotten branch that had fallen from an old pecan tree. Underneath it was a thick covering of dead leaves, whereas there were few leaves at all elsewhere in the area. It was as if someone had scraped the leaves together and put the tree limb on top of them.

Rhodes moved the dead branch aside and kicked away some of the leaves. The dirt beneath them didn't look much different from the dirt on either side, except that in places it seemed just a little darker.

Blood? Rhodes wondered. Could be. Lige could have been shot right on this spot. Rhodes would have to get some soil samples and have them checked. It might not help him find Lige's killer, but any information he could get would be a help.

He went back to his car, got a couple of evidence bags, and dug some of the soil up with his pocket knife. He put the earth in the bags and sealed them, then wrote the information on the tags.

After that, he kept looking. Not far away he found a bush with several broken limbs. It looked almost as if someone had fallen into the bush. The leaves and sticks around it looked disturbed, but Rhodes really couldn't tell much from them. For all he knew, their appearance might have been natural.

But maybe not. There could have been a struggle. The whole area looked suspicious, now that Rhodes was eyeing it more critically. It was as if someone had taken a lot of trouble to make it look as if there hadn't been a struggle there.

Rhodes's ankle was hurting a little, so he walked over to a thick-bodied pecan tree and sat down, resting his back against the trunk. He was beginning to put together in his mind a picture of what might have happened on the night Lige was killed.

Lige had gone to Press Yardley's and taken the emus. If Yardley was telling the truth, he had either been with Rayjean or the dog hadn't alerted him. Either way, he didn't know that anyone had been there until the next day.

Lige might have needed the money the emus would bring him, but it was just as likely he saw stealing them as a way to get a little revenge against Press Yardley.

After loading the emus into his pickup, maybe getting kicked in the chest while doing so, Lige drove over to King's. He unloaded the birds there.

Then King had paid him, or not paid him, and Lige had driven to the cockpit, where someone had shot him and taken the money—if Lige had gotten the money in the first place.

Had it been King who had done the shooting? Why not

shoot Lige at the emu pens if he was going to stuff him in the portable toilet? It would have been much easier that way.

And what about the pistol? Apparently Michael Ferrin had picked it up somewhere near the portable toilet. Had King or someone else dropped it there?

It seemed to Rhodes that whoever had shot Lige would have made a pretty diligent search for the pistol if he dropped it, but maybe not. Maybe the killer was too scared by what had happened to stick around and look for the pistol.

Nard King didn't strike Rhodes as being overly panicky. He certainly didn't appear too worried over the fact that he couldn't find any bill of sale for his emus. But that didn't mean he might not panic in a more serious situation.

In Rhodes's estimation, Wally Henry wouldn't panic at all.

Press Yardley, on the other hand, probably would.

But if the person who shot Lige had panicked, who had put the leaves and the tree branch over the dirt?

There was an answer to that question, and it came to Rhodes quickly.

The person who had shot Lige came back. Rayjean had surprised him, and he had killed her.

Would Press Yardley have killed her, even to cover up murder? Why not? Rhodes had only Yardley's word that Rayjean and the former antique dealer had been having an affair. Yardley could have confessed to confuse the issue.

Wally Henry was certainly lying about several things, and Nard King was almost certainly lying about the emus. Why shouldn't Press Yardley be lying, too? He'd lied about going for groceries; there was no reason he couldn't be lying again. Maybe Hal Keene was lying as well.

And then there was the filed gaff he'd found in Lige's pants. Where did that fit in? Or did it? Maybe Lige had been carrying it around, planning to slip it into a fight when the time seemed right. It was a puzzler, all right.

In all the stories Rhodes had listened to, in all the things he'd found out, Rhodes was sure there was something that would give the killer away, some little thing that wouldn't show up on Hack's computer and couldn't be located in all the files that Hack had access to. All Rhodes had to do was sort out the stories and figure out what that little thing was.

His mind didn't seem to work quite as fast as the computer, nor as efficiently, so it might take him a while. But he was sure he would get to the answer sooner or later.

Rhodes sat there under the tree and looked around. He might not be getting any closer to a solution to the murders, but it was nice just to sit there out of the sun and relax for a minute.

He could hear something scraping in the leaves a little distance behind him—a raccoon maybe, or an armadillo—and there was a squirrel sitting and watching him from about twenty yards away, its head tilted to one side.

Aside from that there was nothing to hear and no other living thing to see. There was no noise from the road, and even the guineas were quiet. There were just the trees and the heat and the shade. Rhodes could almost imagine that he was back in a simpler time, when there weren't any big discount centers sitting on the edge of small towns next to huge supermarkets, their parking lots filled with cars while the former business district stood deserted; a time when men didn't start stealing their neighbor's emus out of a need for money or a need to prove they were still capable of some kind of action.

Rhodes pushed himself away from the tree and stood up. The squirrel scurried away, and Rhodes watched it disappear behind a tree. His ankle was feeling better now. He started back to the county car.

It was all right to feel nostalgic every once in a while, he thought, but there was no use getting carried away. Even before the discount stores had come in, the small towns had been dying. And people had been stealing from their neighbors as long as there had been people and neighbors. Otherwise there wouldn't have ever been a need for sheriffs.

Rhodes got in the car. He thought he'd better go talk to Nard King.

13

JOE BATES AND HIS CREW WERE MAKING GOOD PROGRESS ON King's new house. Rhodes could hear the hammers banging as he got out of his car.

King wasn't anywhere in sight. He didn't seem to be the kind who had to supervise every movement of the men who were working for him. Rhodes went to the old house where King was staying and knocked.

It wasn't long before King was looking out through the screen.

"Oh," he said. "It's you."

"You must've forgotten to call me about those bills of sale," Rhodes said. "So I thought I'd better stop by and have a look at them."

"Don't have 'em," King said. He didn't offer to open the screen. "I've looked all over the place. Can't find hide nor hair of 'em."

"Did you look in all your drawers?" Rhodes asked.

"Drawers?"

"You said you stuck things in drawers," Rhodes reminded him. "That's why you can't find them sometimes."

"Oh. Yeah. I do that, all right. But I looked. Looked in ever' drawer in the house. Didn't find 'em."

"Well, that really doesn't matter," Rhodes said. He took a pad and pencil out of his pocket. "You can just tell me who you bought them from. I'll get in touch with the original owner and verify the sale."

"Can't do that," King said.

"Why not?"

" 'Cause I don't have to do that. Not unless you got good cause to think those emus are stolen, I don't. You got anybody that can identify 'em? Got anybody can point out any identifying marks?"

Rhodes didn't have anyone who could do any of those things, and he suspected that King knew it. Emus all looked pretty much alike, and even if Press Yardley swore that he recognized the birds, there was no way he could prove it.

"Well, Sheriff?" King said.

"There's something else," Rhodes said.

"What's that?"

"You never asked much about Lige Ward's murder. Maybe you haven't heard where his body was found."

Nearly everyone else in the county had heard, of course, but King was a newcomer. He wouldn't be plugged into the gossip circuit yet, and he didn't pal around with the workmen.

"That's right," King said, confirming Rhodes's suspicion. "I haven't heard. Don't know that it's any of my business, either."

"It was in a portable toilet," Rhodes said. "The one that was stolen from your yard." He turned and pointed to the outhouse that had been hauled out to replace the stolen one. "Right over there."

King seemed to shrink in on himself just a little. He pushed open the screen door.

"I guess you'd better come in," he said.

They sat at the same card table they'd sat at during Rhodes's first visit. Only the book on the table was different, though not very different. The new one was called *The Turncoat,* and the cover looked pretty much like the one on the other book King had been reading.

"Just because you found a body in that outhouse doesn't mean I had anything to do with it," King said. "It wasn't *my* outhouse."

"I know that," Rhodes told him. "I was just thinking, though. What if a man stole some emus for me and then I didn't want to pay him? We might get in a fight."

"You sayin' Ward stole emus?" King asked. "Not for me, he didn't. I bought those birds fair and square."

"I'm just thinking aloud."

"Anyway, Lige Ward was a sight bigger than me. I'd never try to fight a fella that big."

Rhodes looked at King's well-muscled arms. "You get in pretty good shape unloading freight for a few years."

"Not in good enough shape to fight a man the size of Ward."

"You have a few years on him. Sometimes that's enough for a good little man to beat a good big man."

King reached out and put a hand on the book. "You even think about writin' fiction, Sheriff?"

"Or maybe you didn't have a fight," Rhodes said. "Maybe when Lige was unloading the emus, he dropped a pistol and didn't know it. You could have picked it up, followed him home, and shot him. That would be a good way to get your money back."

"I didn't shoot him, Sheriff, no matter what you think. Those stories of yours are just getting wilder and wilder. This guy could learn a few things from you."

King held up the book for Rhodes's inspection. The author's name was Adam Rutledge.

"I know you had Lige steal those emus," Rhodes said.

"I never did. You don't have any proof of that, so you might as well leave me alone."

Rhodes felt just about as frustrated as he ever had, but King was right. There just wasn't any proof. That was the trouble with this whole case. There wasn't any proof of anything.

Rhodes drove back to the jail. Hack and Lawton were watching *The Young and the Restless,* but Hack snapped off the TV set when he noticed that Rhodes was looking at them.

Rhodes didn't say anything about the TV. "Did Ruth call in?"

"More'n once," Hack said. "She didn't find anybody that'd seen that GMC."

That was too bad. Rhodes had really hoped to put Wally Henry on the scene.

"Any trouble today?" he asked.

"Not that much," Hack said. "We had a few calls, but nothing that Ruth couldn't handle."

"Little case of desertion," Lawton said quickly, before Hack could get it in.

Hack stared at him.

Rhodes sighed and sat down at his desk. "You want to tell me about it?"

"Nothin' to it," Hack said. "It wasn't really desertion. Got a call from a woman at Terry's Shell Station out on the highway."

"It was abandonment, then," Lawton said. "She said she'd been abandoned."

"I'm the one answered the phone," Hack said. "I guess I know what she said."

Rhodes wished he hadn't asked. He could just have read Ruth's report later. But since he *had* asked, he had to carry through.

"What did she say, then?"

"She said she'd been abandoned," Hack told him.

That was exactly what Lawton had said, of course, but Rhodes didn't bother to point that out. It wouldn't have done any good.

"Who abandoned her?" he asked.

"Her husband," Lawton and Hack said together, each trying to beat the other.

They looked at one another for a few seconds. Lawton blinked first.

"It was her husband," Hack said. "He's the one who abandoned her."

"At Terry's?" Rhodes said. It seemed like a strange place to abandon anyone.

"He didn't really abandon her," Hack said. "Forgot her, is more like it."

"She went to the rest room," Lawton explained. "And he paid up and drove off without her."

"She felt like she needed the sheriff's office for something like that?" Rhodes asked.

"Well," Hack said, "it looked like he wasn't going to come back."

"Yeah," Lawton said. "But he did."

" 'Cause we called the highway boys," Hack said. "That's why. They caught up with him and told him he'd forgot something. That was the first he'd thought of her. He turned right around, of course, but he'd already been gone nearly an hour, and it was another hour before he got back to Terry's."

"If it'd been me, I don't know if I'd've come back," Lawton said. "I think he should've just kept on going." He looked over at Hack. " 'Course I don't know as much about women as some people here."

"You sure don't," Hack said. "But this time you're right about it. He'd've been better off to just keep movin' on. I don't know where those two were headed, but I bet it's gonna be the longest drive that fella ever took."

"At least if he turns up dumped out by the side of the

road, dead in the bar ditch, we'll know who to look for to arrest," Lawton said. "Ain't that right, Sheriff?"

Rhodes agreed that he was right. It was too bad finding out who killed Lige Ward wasn't that easy.

Rhodes talked again to Wally Henry, but Henry was as obstinate as ever. Rhodes knew he wasn't going to get anything from Henry, who would no doubt be bonded out soon. The sheriff needed a break, but he wasn't getting any.

Rhodes spent the rest of the morning and early afternoon catching up on reports, both writing and reading them. Then Hack got a call from Bill Weathers, who said his bull was missing. He wanted someone to come out to investigate.

"Ruth's out down around Thurston," Hack said. "I guess you could go, if you want to."

"Somebody has to," Rhodes said.

Hack didn't see why. "You seen Weathers's fence line lately?"

Rhodes admitted that he hadn't, or if he had, he hadn't noticed it.

"Posts're saggin', wires're all loose, some of 'em draggin' the ground. That bull's not missin'. It's prob'ly out roamin' the road. Next thing you know, there'll be a wreck called in, and there'll be one dead bull."

"Whose pasture is next to Weathers's on the side where the fence is so bad?"

"Lemme see." Hack thought about it. "On that side, it's Milt Pugh."

"Pugh run any cattle?"

"Yeah, and I can see what you're gettin' at. Might be more fun over there than out in the road. Well, that's a registered bull Bill has. I guess Milt won't be makin' any complaints about the calves he gets. You goin' out there anyhow?"

"Have to keep the voters happy," Rhodes said.

* * *

On the way out of town, Rhodes drove past McDonald's. The golden arches were located on the highway only a couple of blocks from Wal-Mart, another example of progress in Clearview, and they reminded Rhodes that he hadn't had any lunch.

It was too late to go home for a healthy slice of wheat bread, he told himself. What could be easier than to drive by the McDonald's window and pick up a burger and some fries? Sure, he'd eaten that sandwich at Hod Barrett's store yesterday, and, yes, he'd gone to the Jolly Tamale last night, but he'd had so much exercise, he must certainly have burned off all the extra calories he'd consumed.

The rationalization was satisfying, but the burger wasn't. Rhodes kept thinking how much better the hamburgers had been when he was a kid. They were thick and hot and greasy, wrapped in some kind of plain white paper. This one was tasteless and bland, though the fries weren't bad.

Rhodes finished the burger and drove on to Bill Weathers's place. He told himself that he was going to have to stop thinking about the way things used to be. The next thing he knew, he'd be chaining himself to the doors at McDonald's.

It took Rhodes about twenty minutes to locate Weathers's bull, who was looking pretty content among Milt Pugh's herd of white-face heifers. He helped Weathers drive the bull back to the right pasture and then admonished Weathers to get his fence fixed.

"Milt Pugh might be the next one to call me," Rhodes said. "Or he might decide to shoot him a bull. If that doesn't happen, somebody might run into him and sue you. From the looks of your fence, they'd have a mighty good case."

That wasn't what Weathers wanted to hear, but he agreed to take care of his fence right away.

Rhodes was on his way back to Clearview when Hack came on the radio.

"Miz McGee's here at the jail," he told Rhodes. "She wants to talk to you."

"What about?"

There was a pause, and Rhodes thought he could hear Hack and Miz McGee talking in the background, though there was a good deal of static on the radio and he couldn't be sure.

After a few seconds, Hack said, "It's about roosters."

"I'll be there in five minutes," Rhodes said.

He didn't speed, but all the same it didn't take him quite that long.

Miz McGee looked the same as always, and Rhodes wondered how she could stand the heat with the wool cap and the sweater. Maybe her metabolism wasn't like everyone else's.

Lawton was the first to see Rhodes come through the door, so he got in the opening remarks.

"Miz McGee's been doin' a little private detective work," he said.

"She can talk for herself," Hack said. "You're always tryin' to hog the glory."

"What glory?" Lawton asked. "All she did was talk to some rooster-fighters."

"That's more'n you did," Hack pointed out.

"Is not. I talked to Gad Pullens. He just wouldn't tell me anything. I don't remember you bringin' in any information the sheriff could use."

Rhodes interrupted them. "Never mind all that. I want to hear what Mrs. McGee has to say."

She was sitting quietly in a cane-bottomed chair next to Hack's desk watching a rerun of "People's Court," paying no attention to Hack's and Lawton's argument.

Rhodes rolled his desk chair over and sat down beside

her. She reluctantly turned away from the TV set. Judge Wapner seemed to interest her a lot more than any case Rhodes might be involved in.

"Now," Rhodes said when he had her attention, "what did you have to tell me?"

Mrs. McGee tugged on her sweater. "Hack was talkin' to me the other day about the cockfights. He said you were lookin' for somebody who knew about things like that." She turned to Hack. "That's right, isn't it?"

"That's right," Hack said. "You go ahead and tell the sheriff what you found out."

She turned back to Rhodes. "Well, I know this woman, Polly Fisher. Her husband, his name's Curtis, has a fightin' rooster. So I talked to her. She told me Curtis was at a rooster fight at Lige Ward's not so long ago."

She paused as if waiting for either approval or permission to go on.

"That's exactly the kind of information I was looking for," Rhodes said. "Did she say anything else?"

"She told me there was a big fight that day. Lige had to break it up."

Rhodes was a little confused for a moment, but then he sorted it out.

"You mean there was a fight between the men, not the roosters?"

"That's right. One of the men was terrible upset. Killin' mad, she said. Curtis told her he'd never seen anything like it in his life."

"What was the fight about?" Rhodes asked.

"She didn't tell me that. I don't think she knows. Curtis didn't want to talk much about it. Just said how awful it was, and that was all. She didn't want him goin' to any more cockfights, and he told her he'd do what he pleased."

Rhodes asked a question before she got too far off track.

"Did she say who that man was? The one who got so mad?"

"Yes, she did. Curtis told her that much. It was a man named Wally Henry."

Rhodes looked at Hack, who was shaking his head.

"Bonded out over an hour ago," he said. "Got him a ride and went home."

14

MRS. MCGEE HADN'T BEEN ABLE TO FIND OUT WITH WHOM Wally Henry had fought.

"Just some young fella Curtis didn't know," she said.

She also didn't think that Curtis would talk to the sheriff or anybody else about what had happened.

"Polly asked me not to tell Curtis that she'd talked to me. Curtis don't like folks to know he goes to rooster fights. You won't have to tell him, will you?"

Rhodes said he'd keep Curtis out of things if he could, but he wasn't making any promises. He was getting a little tired of people who were trying to cover up their illegal activities.

But even if he kept Curtis Fisher's secret, just knowing about that fight was something to think about. Rhodes wondered why Clyde hadn't mentioned it.

He thanked Mrs. McGee for her time and for getting the information for him. Then he left on another trip to Thurston.

He now had three people who had seen Wally Henry at the cockfight, if you counted both Clyde and Claude. It was possible that Hal Keene had seen Henry as well. Rhodes had already been sure that Henry was lying about not having been there, but the fight was something new. Clyde hadn't said a thing about it, and neither had Keene, though Keene probably hadn't hung around long enough to see it. Maybe the twins hadn't either, but then again maybe they had. With them, you could never be too sure about what they knew and what they didn't know.

Rhodes drove into Henry's yard and parked by the GMC. Henry was with the roosters, but he left them as soon as he saw the county car. He moved fast and was beside the car almost before Rhodes could get out.

"Look here, Sheriff," Henry said. "You can just get right back in that car and get off my property. I've paid my bail and you don't have any business with me now."

"Yes, I do," Rhodes said. "I have three eyewitnesses who'll swear that they saw you at Lige Ward's cockfight. You lied about that."

Rhodes was doing some lying of his own now, since it was far from a certainty that any of the three he was thinking of would swear to anything, but he figured it was about time he took the offensive. He was tired of pussyfooting around. If Curtis Fisher didn't want to go to court and swear whom he'd seen at a cockfight, that was just too bad. And the same went for Claude and Clyde. Hal Keene, too, if it came to that.

"Eyewitnesses?" Henry said. "I don't b'lieve it. Bring 'em on. I got a right to face my accusers."

"Not until we get to court," Rhodes said. "They also tell me you got in a fight with somebody there."

"Buncha damn liars is what they are," Henry said, but Rhodes detected a slight quaver in the high voice.

Rhodes pressed his advantage. "In fact, you got in a fight at the Palm Club, and Lige Ward had to break that one up, too. It seems to me you're getting in an awful lot of fights lately. And it seems mighty convenient that Lige Ward is always there to break them up. Now I want to know two things. Who were you fighting with, and why?"

"I don't have to tell you a damn thing." Henry turned his back on Rhodes and started to walk toward his stags. "I got some roosters to take care of."

"Just a minute," Rhodes said. "I'm not through talking to you."

Henry stopped, but he didn't turn back. He just stood there, and for a while Rhodes thought the big man wasn't ever going to move again. Finally he made up his mind, though. He turned around and faced Rhodes.

His face was pinched and his eyes were hard. "Let me tell you somethin', Sheriff."

"Go ahead. I wish you would."

"I'm not so sure you want to hear what I have to say. What I want to tell you is this. Whoever I fight with is my business. It don't have diddly to do with Lige Ward. It has to do with me and the man I'm mad at."

"Lige Ward got killed the same night he broke up one of your fights," Rhodes said. "Don't you care about Lige?"

Henry shrugged his wide shoulders. "Why should I? I didn't ask him to butt in. He's lucky I didn't whip his ass while I was at it."

"You've got a bad temper, Wally. Maybe you're the one who killed him."

"Well, I ain't. Lige never done anything to me 'cept stick his nose in where it wasn't needed a couple of times. I'd never kill a man that never hurt me. I might whip him, but I'd never kill him." He paused and gave Rhodes a hard look. "But if a man cheated me, then I'd kill him. If I got the chance. But I wouldn't do it where you could ever find out about it."

Rhodes didn't know whether it was what Henry said or the way he said it. Maybe it wasn't either one. Maybe it was simply that everything he'd thought about and all the things he'd been told by everyone he'd talked to just shuffled around in his head at that point and suddenly all the pieces fell into their proper places.

He thought he knew who'd killed the Wards and why it had been done.

Thinking he knew was one thing. Proving it, however, was something different.

"I guess a lot of people feel like killing somebody at one time or another," he told Henry. "You're probably going to have to testify to that in court, by the way."

"To what? That I'd kill a man that cheated me? I'd like to see you make me." There was no quaver in Henry's voice this time.

"I can make you. You'll be subpoenaed, and if you don't appear, I'll come after you. You can testify in handcuffs just as well as not."

"You're bluffin'," Henry said.

"You wish," Rhodes said. "You go take care of your roosters now. I'll be seeing you again."

"Don't be in no big hurry about it," Henry said, but Rhodes could tell he knew he'd lost.

Back at the jail, Rhodes gathered up some photographs. He could still be wrong, but he didn't think he was. Nevertheless, he had to get some corroboration before he went out and arrested anyone.

"You been thinkin' about what I said?" Hack asked him.

"About what?" Rhodes wanted to know.

" 'Bout them video cameras. See, if you had one in your car, and you didn't come back from Wally Henry's place, we could run down there to Thurston and recover the car. Then we'd take out the tape and run it on a VCR and see if he chopped you up and fed you to the roosters."

"What if he took the camera? Or just took out the tape? After he fed me to the roosters, I mean. A man like that might even torch the car."

Hack gave Rhodes a sorrowful look. "That's just the way you are. Always lookin' for the weak points. But we could prob'ly get him for theft if he did that. Maybe for destruction of county property, too. Wouldn't you rest easier knowin' that the fella that murdered you'd been brought to justice by the miracle of modern technology?"

"I'd still be rooster food," Rhodes pointed out. "There's not much comfort in that."

"Yeah, but the fella that did you in 'ud be in the clink. Justice 'ud be served."

Rhodes didn't see it that way. "For stealing a camera? How long do you think he'd be in? And you probably couldn't prove he stole it anyway. He might get off scot-free."

"I swear," Hack said, "you're just about the worst I ever saw for not ever wantin' to change things."

"I haven't chained myself to any discount-center doors yet," Rhodes said.

Hack muttered something about it just being a matter of time, but Rhodes didn't stop to argue with him. He had other things on his mind.

Like identifying a killer.

The warehouse at Wal-Mart wasn't a particularly busy place late in the afternoon. Clyde and Claude were there, but they weren't doing much. It seemed to Rhodes that they were just trying to look busy, even though there was no work for them.

He ignored them and went straight to Keene's office, but Keene wasn't there. A woman came over from the break table to see if she could help Rhodes.

"Mr. Keene's on the floor," she said. "Is there something the matter, Sheriff?"

"Not a thing," Rhodes assured her. "I just need to talk to Mr. Keene for a second."

"I'll call him," she said.

She went into Keene's office and paged him on the store's intercom system. He showed up in under a minute.

"I'll handle this, Mary," he said, dismissing the woman who had paged him.

She went back over to the break table and sat down, plainly disappointed. Rhodes could see that she was very interested in what was going on, but she was too well trained to ask.

"Well, Sheriff?" Keene said.

"We'd better go in your office," Rhodes told him.

Keene's shoulders slumped just a little, but he went inside without saying another word. Rhodes followed him in and closed the door behind him.

"I hope this isn't about what I think it is," Keene said, sitting behind his desk.

"It is," Rhodes said.

"I guess I should've expected it. I tell you, Sheriff, I wish to God I'd never seen a rooster. Does my wife have to know?"

"It's not as bad as all that," Rhodes said. "All I want you to do is look at some pictures."

Keene cheered up. "Pictures? Why?"

"I want to see if you recognize anyone in them."

Keene didn't mind that at all. He was almost smiling as Rhodes spread the photographs on the desk.

"Look at them carefully," he said. "Take your time. Then point out anyone you recognize."

"Where am I supposed to have seen these people?" Keene asked.

"I'd just as soon leave that up to you, if you don't mind," Rhodes said. "You just look and see who you recognize, and maybe you can say where you saw them."

Keene stared at the pictures for at least a minute. He pushed a couple of them around with his index finger. Rhodes was beginning to wonder if his hunch was going to pay off.

Then Keene picked up one of the photographs to look at

it more carefully. He held it close to his face and squinted his eyes. Then he pushed it out almost to arm's length.

"I might know this one," he said.

"What's his name?"

"I wouldn't know that. I only saw him once, if he's the one I think he is."

"Where did you see him, then?"

"At the cockfight," Keene said. "At Lige Ward's."

That was the answer Rhodes had been hoping for, but he didn't let it get him too excited. Now he wanted some more confirmation.

"Would you mind letting me talk to the Appleby boys in here?" he asked. "Privately?"

"Not at all. Are they in some kind of trouble?"

"No," Rhodes said. "I just have to ask them a few questions, just like I had to ask you a few. I wouldn't want you to think they'd done anything wrong. They haven't."

"I'll get them for you then. Is there anything else you want from me?"

"That's all. You did fine."

"And you're not going to tell my wife?"

"Not yet, anyway," Rhodes said.

Might as well let Keene sweat a little, he thought. Maybe Keene would think twice before he got mixed up in activities that he knew perfectly well were illegal.

He might have known that he wasn't out of the woods yet, but Keene nevertheless got up and went out of the office with a lighter step than he had entered. In a few seconds Clyde and Claude were at the door.

"You want us?" Claude asked.

Rhodes was pretty sure it was Claude, at any rate. The twins were wearing jeans and identical blue shirts, along with their Wal-Mart vests. They looked more alike than ever to Rhodes.

"I'll take you first," Rhodes said. "Clyde, you can wait outside."

The twin who had spoken came inside the office. Right again, Rhodes thought. Either that, or the twins were just humoring him. He didn't care. He didn't think it mattered much one way or the other.

"You can close the door," Rhodes told him.

When he had done so, Claude asked, "Is this gonna get us in any trouble with Mr. Keene? You didn't tell him what Clyde said about him being at the cockfight, did you?"

Rhodes answered the second question first. "I didn't tell him who saw him there, and he didn't ask. And you don't have to worry about getting into trouble. I've taken care of that already."

Claude nodded. "Okay."

Rhodes showed him the photos on the desk. "I'd like for you to take a look at those. See if there's anyone there you've seen before."

It didn't take Claude as long as it had taken Keene. He picked up the same picture that the manager had chosen.

"I've seen this one."

"Do you remember where?"

"He was at that cockfight where we saw Mr. Keene."

"All right," Rhodes said. He took the photo from Claude and laid it on the desk. "Did you see anything else that day, anything you haven't mentioned to me?"

Claude shrugged. "Like what?"

"Like a fight between two of the men. A fight that Lige Ward had to break up."

Claude looked up at the low ceiling of the little office. Then he looked off to the side.

"Well?" Rhodes asked.

Claude turned his head but not enough for him to be looking directly at Rhodes. It was as if he were looking at a point just to the left of the sheriff's shoulder.

"Okay," he said, "there was this fight. But me and Clyde don't know what it was about. We were too far off to hear.

The guy you asked about, you know, the one with the pigtail?"

"What about him?"

"He was in on it, him and the guy in the picture." Claude pointed to the photo Rhodes had taken from him. "They went at it pretty good, and the guy in the pigtail was gettin' the best of it before Mr. Ward broke it up. There was a lot of yellin' after that, and there weren't any more cockfights. Ever'body got in their cars and went home. Me and Clyde hung around awhile, and then we went home too."

"What about Mr. Keene?"

"He was there, too. Just like Clyde told you."

"During the fight?"

"No, not then. He left pretty quick after he got there. I think he was afraid somebody'd see him. He kept to the back of the crowd, and he kept lookin' around like he was worried about somethin'."

"You'd swear to all that in court?" Rhodes asked.

"I don't know about that. I don't much like courts."

"Maybe you won't have to. You can go on back to work now. I'll see what Clyde has to say."

"He'll say the same as I did."

"I don't doubt it," Rhodes told him.

It turned out pretty much the way Claude had predicted. Clyde told almost the same story, but he did add that most of the yelling that had gone on had been between the two men involved in the fight rather than anyone else who was there.

And he had heard a little bit more than Claude had been willing to admit to.

"The guy with the pigtail said he was going to kill the other fella," Clyde said. "He said the other fella was a sorry son of—"

"Never mind," Rhodes said. "I get the idea. Did he have a weapon? A knife or a gun?"

"Not that I saw," Clyde said. "But if he wanted to, he was big enough to do it barehanded."

"He didn't, though."

"Nope." Clyde sounded almost disappointed. "He didn't do anything. Mr. Ward was holdin' him back by that time. Then he sorta got calmed down, and the other guy and his buddies left. Ever'body else did, too. They all walked back through the woods and drove off."

"Why did they walk through the woods?"

"All their cars were parked out on that little road that runs along in back of the property there."

Claude was talking about the same road where Brother Alton had been parked when Rhodes spotted his Cadillac pulling away from the fence.

"I guess Mr. Ward didn't like the idea of ever'body comin' in through his front gate," Clyde went on. "Somebody might wonder what they were doin' there."

"Wouldn't people see the cars along the side of that back road?" Rhodes asked.

Clyde shook his head. "Nobody ever goes along there. Maybe one car a day. Hardly anybody lives along back that way. Anybody did go by there would know what was goin' on and keep their mouth shut."

Rhodes figured that was true. If he hadn't seen the Cadillac pulling away, no one would ever have reported its being there. Either no one would have been suspicious or no one would have cared.

"It seems like everybody in the county knew about that cockfight but me," Rhodes said.

"Yes, sir," Clyde said. He was experienced in such matters. "That sounds about right. Sheriff's not supposed to know about stuff like that."

"I'll know if it happens again," Rhodes said.

"Maybe so, but it won't happen in this county now that they know you're on to 'em. They'll just move somewhere across the line. I bet they fight ever' week in the country round Stassen."

Stassen was the county seat of the neighboring county. Rhodes knew the sheriff there pretty well.

"Do you know something you should be telling me?" he asked.

"Not a thing," Clyde said.

Rhodes looked at the boy's bland face. If he hadn't known better, he might even have believed him.

Rhodes sat in Keene's office and looked over the photographs before putting them in his pocket. He was now certain that he was right about who had killed the Wards, but proving his presence at the cockfight didn't mean a thing. It was certainly nothing that would hold up in a law court. What Rhodes needed was some hard evidence, some kind of proof that a good defense lawyer couldn't get a jury to disregard.

And Rhodes didn't have that kind of proof.

He wondered where he could find it.

15

▼

BACK AT THE JAIL HACK AND LAWTON WERE WATCHING THE last few minutes of "Geraldo." Rhodes gathered it was a show about mothers who stole their daughters' husbands.

"Watching that stuff will rot your brains," Rhodes warned them.

"We know that," Lawton said. "But you gotta admit, it's kinda fascinatin'."

"Educational is what it is," Hack said. "You think we got any of that kind of thing goin' on around here?"

"There was that Miz Hawkins," Lawton said. "Lived on Plum Street."

"I remember her," Hack said. "Musta been sixty if she was a day."

"Not as old as some women I could name," Lawton said.

"You better not be talkin' about Miz McGee," Hack warned him. "I told you 'bout that."

"I was just talkin' in general," Lawton said. "I just meant to say that sixty ain't all that old."

"That better be it."

"That's it. I didn't mean a thing. Anyway, she run off with her oldest daughter's husband. You remember that, don't you, Sheriff?"

Rhodes remembered, all right. "The daughter turned in a missing-person's report on them," he said.

"That's right," Hack chimed in. "But it turned out they weren't missin' at all, just gone off on a little lovers' honeymoon."

"Little?" Lawton said. "Didn't they go to Hawaii?" He pronounced it "High-wah-yah."

"Honolulu," Rhodes said. "We traced them through the travel agency."

"See how good those computers are?" Hack asked. "Make all those records real easy to get at. Now a TV camera in the county cars—"

"Never mind that," Rhodes said. "Get Deputy Grady on the radio. I need to talk to her."

"On the radio or in person?" Hack asked.

"In person," Rhodes said. "Have her come in."

"I'll do that," Hack said. He turned to the radio. Then he turned back. "You know, I bet there was a sheriff or two back in the old days that, when the radio came in, they said, 'No, thanks, boys. No radio for me. I'd just as soon do things the old way, send out somebody to find whoever it is I want. We don't need none of those newfangled gadgets around here at *my* jail.' "

"Are you going to call her or not?" Rhodes asked.

"I'll call her," Hack said. "It's just that I was thinkin' how hard it is to hold back progress. Like those TV cameras ever'body's gettin' these days."

"Hack," Rhodes said.

Yes, sir," Hack said. "I'm callin' her right now, Mr. Sheriff."

Rhodes sighed and said nothing.

Ruth brought out the casts she'd made at Press Yardley's emu pens and explained to Rhodes what she had.

"Press Yardley wears a pair of old Nike waffle-soled jogging shoes most of the time," she said. "They're easy to spot." She showed Rhodes the cast and held up another one. "This one's you, and you've already seen Mr. Ward's."

"And that was all?" Rhodes asked. "Didn't you mention something about boots?"

"Well, there's this one." Ruth held up a casting that Rhodes could see was incomplete. "It doesn't match anybody."

"It wouldn't be much good in court, then," Rhodes said.

"It would be all right if we could find a perfect match for it. There's nothing like there was on Mr. Ward's shoe, but you can see that there's a little mark in the sole, where a rock cut it, maybe."

"We could prove it was the same size as someone's foot, too, couldn't we?"

"Sure. But that wouldn't be enough."

"I didn't think so. What about the fingerprints on the portable outhouse?"

"That was a hopeless job," Ruth said. "There were fingerprints all over the place, most of them smudged. But even if there were some good prints, what could you take to court? There'd been workmen using it for weeks, it had been put in that truck by three men, and even you touched it. No good lawyer would let something like that get by."

That didn't leave them much. They were going to have to find a boot to match the print, and even that wouldn't prove that the owner of the boot had shot Lige Ward.

"So what are we going to do?" Ruth asked.

"Bluff," Rhodes said. "That's about all we've got left."

"What if that doesn't work?"

"We'll try lying," Rhodes said. "Everybody else does it. But first I'll have a little talk with Curtis Fisher."

Fisher was a mechanic at a small auto repair shop that didn't close until the day's work was done. Although it was after five by the time Rhodes got there, the shop was still open.

It was a high-roofed corrugated tin building with tall garage doors on both sides. There were two large fans in wire cages, one at each end of the building, humming and pushing the hot air around. The concrete floor was covered with dark stains, and most of the light came through the open doors.

Curtis Fisher was a dried-up little man whose snuff-colored skin made him look as if he spent most of his time outside rather than inside a garage.

A trouble light hung from beneath the hood of an old Plymouth Fury and illuminated Fisher's features as he poked around under there. There was an oil-stained red cloth on the fender beside him. A socket wrench and three spark plugs were lying on the cloth.

While Rhodes watched, Fisher took the wrench and tightened a plug that he had begun screwing into place with his fingers. When he finished, he put the wrench back on the cloth and turned to Rhodes.

"Yessir, Sheriff. What can I do for you? One of the county cars actin' up?"

"We're not having car trouble," Rhodes said. "I just wanted to talk to you."

Fisher looked around the garage. There was one other mechanic who worked in the shop, but he was nowhere to be seen.

"What about?" Fisher asked.

"I've been trying to talk to all the men who were at that cockfight at Lige Ward's place," Rhodes told him. "You're one of them."

"Who told you that?"

"Like I said, I'm talking to everyone who was there. Several of them mentioned you."

Fisher picked up the socket wrench and slapped it into his palm a couple of times. Then he laid it back down.

"People talk too much," he said.

"Or not enough," Rhodes said. "Cockfights are against the law."

"That mean you're goin' to arrest me?"

"Not this time. I'm just looking for information."

"I don't like talkin' about folks. What they do is their own business if they ain't hurtin' nobody else. A little rooster fight don't hurt anybody."

Rhodes didn't see any need to mention what it did to the roosters. Fisher would have the same view as Wally Henry, and Rhodes had heard that already. Some minds couldn't be changed.

"People can get hurt if they get in a fight among themselves," he said. "Sometimes people can even get killed."

"You're talkin' 'bout Lige, I guess."

"That's right."

"He didn't get killed at that rooster fight, if that's what's botherin' you."

"I know that. But there was another fight that day, and it wasn't between two roosters."

Fisher picked up the wrench again. "Oh. Yeah. There was. But it didn't last long. Lige broke it up."

"What was it about?"

"Wally Henry thought he'd been cheated. He lost one of his best roosters."

"Roosters get killed at those fights all the time."

"You'd be surprised. It don't happen all that often."

"But it did this time."

"Sure did. But Wally, he thought it was a cheat."

"Was it?"

"Hell, how would I know?"

"I thought maybe everybody knew," Rhodes said.

"Nobody knew. Lige broke things up, and people looked around some, but there wasn't any proof of anything. 'Course, by then the other fella'd had hold of his rooster for a minute or two. Plenty of time to hide the evidence."

"Who was the other fella, by the way?"

"Don't know," Fisher said. "Never saw him before."

"Now why is it that I don't believe that?" Rhodes asked.

"You might's well."

"I don't think so. I know better. I know that there's not a different crowd every time there's a cockfight. It's the same people, or nearly the same, every single time. There aren't that many who're interested."

Rhodes took his pictures out of his pocket and shuffled through them. Then he held one up.

"Well?" he said.

Fisher looked for a moment as if he weren't going to say anything. Then he started to put the wrench back on the fender. He let go too soon and the wrench slid off the fender to the floor, where it bounced with a clear ringing sound that echoed off the tin walls.

"Okay," he said when the echoes died, "that's him. But I don't know his name, and that's the truth."

"That's all right," Rhodes said. "I do."

Michael Ferrin lived about a half mile out of Clearview at the top of a sandy hill just off the road to Obert. The tires of the county car churned up a white cloud as Rhodes drove up the hill. The car would need washing, but not as badly as the one Ruth was driving along behind him.

Ruth was there because Ivy had insisted after one of Rhodes's recent escapades that he never again go out to make an arrest without backup. He'd nearly been mowed down by a tree-whacker.

Ivy was right, of course, and Rhodes should have been taking backup all along, but with a department the size of Blacklin County's it just wasn't always feasible, especially when Rhodes believed that most of the people he was going to confront would come along with him peacefully.

Unfortunately, the cooperation of felons had not generally lived up to Rhodes's expectations. And he didn't want to wind up being fed to a bunch of roosters, whether they belonged to Wally Henry or Michael Ferrin.

Except that Ferrin didn't have any roosters, at least not any that Rhodes could see. That was too bad, since Rhodes's whole reconstruction of what had happened at the cockfight and afterward depended on Ferrin's having some cocks. Rhodes was sure he remembered seeing feathers in the back of Ferrin's pickup, feathers that could have come from a rooster carried in a cage.

If Ferrin did have any roosters, however, they weren't out in the open like Wally Henry's.

Of course Henry's were stags, not fully grown cocks, or so he said, and therefore there was nothing wrong with having them on display. Real fighting roosters were another matter.

Ferrin's house was set back a short distance from the road. It was a fairly new red brick structure with a wide black satellite dish in the side yard. The Toyota pickup was parked in the garage. Rhodes could see the word YO on the tailgate.

Rhodes eased his car into the driveway and stopped. Ruth Grady parked behind him, and they got out.

"You think he's home?" Ruth asked.

"There's his truck," Rhodes said, pointing to the garage. "And it's after five. He wouldn't still be at work. Maybe he didn't hear us drive up."

"Or maybe he's not in the house," Ruth said. "There's an old barn back there."

Ferrin's house had been built on the site of an older home that had been demolished. There was nothing left of the place except an old well housing that was overgrown with vines and half hidden by a tickle-tongue tree, that and the old barn in back. The barn was made of rusted tin and looked as if a good breeze would blow it over. The tin roof was peeled back in several places, revealing the wooden studs, and a couple of sections of tin were missing altogether.

"Let's go see if he's in the house before we check the barn," Rhodes said.

He went by the garage first and looked into the pickup bed. The beer cans were still there, along with the dirt and the feathers that Rhodes remembered. Rooster feathers, Rhodes was pretty sure.

Feathers, boots, a young man and his buddies at the cockfight, three young men wearing western clothes and talking to Lige at the Palm Club. It all fit together, and it had all led Rhodes to believe that he'd been considering the wrong suspects. There was someone else who'd had contact with Lige, or Lige's dead body, whom Rhodes had been overlooking all along.

He left the truck and went to the front door. Ruth stood behind him near the door. There was a lighted doorbell button, and Rhodes pushed it. He heard a chime sound faintly inside the house. No one came to see who was there.

"I guess you were right about the barn," Rhodes said. "Let's go check it out."

He started around the house. Ruth walked along beside him and drew her sidearm.

"You won't need that," Rhodes said, glancing over at her.

"Maybe not," she said. "But I like to have it handy just in case."

Rhodes didn't say any more. Ruth had pulled him out of a tight spot once, and there had been more than one time when he had wished for a weapon he didn't have.

The barn door was open, and Rhodes could hear the roosters before he got to the barn. There weren't many of them, but he was glad to know they were there. It made him feel better about his theory.

When they reached the barn, Rhodes motioned to Ruth to wait outside. He went through the door and saw Ferrin, who had his back to the door. He was holding a rooster and feeding it something with an eye dropper. The other end of the barn was open, and there was a large object there, covered with a dirty tarp.

"I didn't know you kept roosters," Rhodes said.

Ferrin wheeled around, keeping his grip on the rooster, which looked bug-eyed and frightened, though it didn't make a sound. For all Rhodes knew, all fighting cocks looked that way.

"You ought to know better than to sneak up on a man like that, Sheriff," Ferrin said. His eyes looked a little like the rooster's. "Is this a social call, or do you have something to say to me?"

"I wouldn't say it was a social call," Rhodes said.

"What's it about then?"

"Murder," Rhodes told him.

"Murder? You're joking, right?"

"I'm not joking. You killed Lige Ward, and you killed his wife, Rayjean."

Ferrin took a step forward. "Now wait a minute, Sheriff. You've got the wrong guy. I never killed anybody. Sure, me and the fellas shot up that little outhouse, but that dead man was already in it. We didn't know that."

"I'm not sure about the other two," Rhodes said. "But you did."

It was hot in the barn and dust swirled in the light of the late-afternoon sun that came in through the open spaces in the roof. There was sweat on Ferrin's upper lip.

"You've got me mixed up with somebody else," he said. "I don't know what you're talking about. I was with Kyle and Larry when Ward was shot."

"No, you weren't. I didn't remember until later, but you admitted that you went out to get beer. Those two were so drunk, they didn't know how long you were gone. It's not a five-minute drive from here to Obert. You had time to kill Lige, all right."

"Are you supposed to be asking me this stuff without some kinda warnin'?"

"I'm glad to see that young people take such an interest in the law," Rhodes said.

He got a card from his pocket and read off the Miranda warning. Ferrin listened with amusement.

"Just like on TV. But you're all wrong about me, Sheriff."

"I wish I was. But I'm not. I should've thought of it sooner, when Burl Griffin told me about the three men Wally Henry jumped at the Palm Club. That was the second time Lige had to pull him off you."

"What if he did?" Ferrin asked.

"Wally was mad, but Lige persuaded him to go on home. Then he came back in and talked to you. I think he showed you something like this."

Rhodes pulled the gaff that Lawton had made from his pocket and let Ferrin have a look at it.

"I never saw that before," Ferrin said.

Rhodes thought the rooster's eyes bulged a little more and wondered if Ferrin was squeezing it too tightly. He stuck the gaff back in his pocket.

"He wanted money from you, I guess," Rhodes said. "Either you paid him, or he was going to tell Wally Henry that you used this gaff in the cockfight. Wally was already convinced that you did. That's why he fought with you the first time."

"You've sure got a good imagination, Sheriff," Ferrin said.

"People keep telling me that. I wish I did, but I'm not making any of this up. I should have known it all comes back to the gaff. Why else would Lige have been carrying it?"

"Beats me. Anyway, if I killed Lige, how did I do it?"

Rhodes wasn't too clear on that, but he thought he had a pretty good idea.

"You went by his place after you told your buddies you were going for more beer. Maybe you just wanted to be sure about where he lived. But I think you happened to see him at Press Yardley's emu pens, or maybe at Nard King's. You figured he was up to something illegal, considering the time of night, so you stopped to make a bargain with him. You'd keep quiet if he would. He didn't want to talk where he was and take a chance on getting caught by Yardley or on letting King know that he'd been seen, so he told you to drive on to his place and meet him at the cockpit. When he came, the two of you got in a scuffle, he lost the pistol he was carrying, and you shot him."

Ferrin thought a second and then said, "That's the craziest thing I ever heard."

"Could be. But killing Mrs. Ward was nothing like that."

"Why would I kill her? She wasn't trying to blackmail me like you say her husband was."

"I think it was an accident," Rhodes told him. "I think you switched the gaffs in the pit and hid the filed ones there. Maybe you buried them in the sand. I think Lige found one on each leg, and the day after you killed him, you went back for the other one. Rayjean heard those guineas clattering when you drove by and went to see who was in her woods. Maybe you were scared; maybe you didn't mean to hit her quite so hard. Or maybe you did."

"You sound convinced I did it," Ferrin said.

"I am. You were smart, though. Who'd ever believe that the person who killed Lige would be dumb enough to go shooting at the very outhouse he hid the body in?"

"That's what I say. That's so farfetched, *I* sure don't believe it."

"It took me long enough to catch on," Rhodes said. "I never even considered that you'd done it until I started hearing about Wally Henry fighting a young fella, or three young fellas, at the Palm Club. But it was a pretty good plan. If bullets from that gun were in Lige, well, your pals were with you when you found it. They could vouch for that. All of you were shooting. Naturally a bullet or two might go through the walls. How were your buddies to know you'd planned it all along?"

"I was too drunk to plan anything that night. You know that."

"It had to be that way." Rhodes paused. "You know, if you'd left Lige where he fell, you might've gotten away with it, but I think you were scared. You thought you had to hide the body, and then you realized you hadn't hidden it very well. Besides, your fingerprints might be on the outhouse. After you moved it, that didn't matter so much. There was a reason for them. Just three young guys drinking and having a good time."

"If I'm so smart," Ferrin said, "how did you manage to catch me?"

"You searched Lige's clothes," Rhodes said, "looking for the gaff. You didn't find it, but you left something behind. You left your fingerprints on his wallet."

"I never touched his wallet. And I didn't kill him."

"Then how did your fingerprints get there?" Rhodes asked.

"They didn't," Ferrin said. "You're lying. You're setting me up for somethin' I never did."

"And you killed Mrs. Ward, too. I know that for a fact."

Rhodes knew nothing of the sort, but he figured that while he was lying, he might as well do a good job of it.

"You don't know a thing. You're goin' to get me for a murder I never did!"

Ferrin squeezed the rooster tighter and looked wildly around the barn, as if wondering how he could escape without being stopped by Rhodes.

Rhodes took a step forward and put out his hand. Ferrin yelled and threw the rooster in Rhodes's face.

16

▼

IT'S ALL VERY WELL TO KNOW FOR A NEAR CERTAINTY THAT fighting roosters don't fight human beings. Knowing that fact, however, isn't really much of a comfort when one of them is screeching like a hawk and flying directly at your head.

Rhodes bent down and twisted aside, feeling only a flurry of heat and feathers as the rooster flapped by him. It landed behind him and staggered awkwardly for several feet before righting itself. It fluttered its wings and crowed loudly, as if proud of its accomplishment.

Rhodes turned to see where Ferrin had gone. The young man had run to the open end of the barn and thrown aside the tarp. He was climbing on a red four-wheeled ATV.

The ATV started with a roar just as Ruth Grady entered the barn and fired off a shot in Ferrin's direction. The bullet pinged through the tin side of the barn.

"Don't shoot him," Rhodes yelled.

He wasn't sure Ruth could hear him. His ears were ringing from the shot and the blare of the ATV's engine, and he could hardly hear himself. He started running after Ferrin, who gunned the ATV out the back of the barn.

"Get the car," Rhodes yelled over his shoulder, roosters

bumping against his legs and scrambling to get out of his way as he ran.

By the time Rhodes got out of the barn, Ferrin was well on his way across the small fenced pasture. Rhodes didn't have any hope of catching him on foot, but he kept on running.

The footing wasn't good. The sandy ground was soft, the weeds were high thanks to the recent rain, and there were fire-ant mounds all over the place. The thick weeds tugged at Rhodes's legs as he tried to jog around the fire-ant mounds, and his feet sank into the sandy soil.

Even worse, the pasture had been plowed at some time in the past, and most of the terraces had never leveled out. The ATV was bouncing high, throwing Ferrin up off the seat. Rhodes was stumbling across the rises, and every step was aggravating his sore ankle. The going would be even rougher in the car, but at least it wouldn't hurt his ankle.

Ruth pulled up beside Rhodes after he'd gone about fifty yards. While the car was still moving, he opened the door and jumped in. Ruth pushed the accelerator down hard before he was settled in the seat, and he grabbed for the seat belt as the car bucked along.

"Keep moving," he said.

The car nosed up over a terrace and landed with a *whump* on the other side. Rhodes tried to talk as Ruth fought the wheel.

"There are places"—*whump!* "—we could get stuck"— *whump!* "—in this sand if you"—*whump!* "—slow down too much"—*whump!*

Rhodes gave up. Riding in the car across the pasture was like riding a bronco at the Clearview Rodeo. It wasn't a situation that was favorable to conversation. Rhodes kept thinking his stomach was going to fly out his mouth. Either that or the bottom of his spine was going to punch a hole in the car seat.

There was a gate in the fence that surrounded the pasture,

just barbed wire attached to a movable cedar post. Ferrin jumped off the ATV, opened the gate, got back in the saddle, and zipped through the opening. Ruth went through the gate only seconds behind him. Ferrin hunched over the handlebars of the ATV, rumbling along a rutted road that led downhill, and Ruth followed him. The road wasn't exactly a highway, but the car wasn't bouncing nearly as much as it had in the pasture, for which Rhodes was thankful.

At the bottom of the hill the road leveled out for a few yards before it crossed through a shallow creek bed. The creek was a very small one, not more than ten feet wide, with only a few inches of water in it.

The wide tires of Ferrin's ATV sluiced through the water, throwing up a silvery spray that flashed in the light of the sinking sun, and then Ferrin was bouncing up the other side of the creek bed and headed up another hill, leaving a cloud of sand in his wake. At the top of the hill was a thick stand of woods.

Rhodes wasn't sure that the county car would cross the creek quite as easily as the ATV had, but it was too late to say anything. Ruth had a determined look on her face and wasn't slowing down a bit.

The nose of the car slammed into the shallow water, and if Rhodes hadn't been wearing his seat belt, his head would have hit the roof.

The car nosed out of the creek, and the back wheels spun for a second or two on the slick bottom. Rhodes had a sinking sensation, but then the tires grabbed some traction and the car shot out of the creek and up the hill.

"If he gets to those trees, he's going to get away," Ruth said. "He can maneuver in there, and we can't."

Rhodes reached for his pistol. "Maybe I can shoot out a tire."

"That's what I was trying to do," Ruth said. "In the barn."

Rhodes should have known that she wasn't trying to shoot Ferrin, but he didn't take the time to apologize. He rolled down the window and stuck his arm out, steadying it the best he could with his left hand.

He fired off two quick shots, with no result. He told himself that shooting uphill from a moving car while eating grit would be tricky for anyone.

"Can you catch him before he gets to the trees?" he asked.

"We'll see."

Ruth floored the accelerator. The car didn't exactly jump forward, but it moved faster up the sandy hill.

"Try to get beside him," Rhodes said.

"Are you going to shoot him?"

"No. I'm going to try to jump on him."

"You'll kill yourself," Ruth said.

"Probably," Rhodes agreed. "Randolph Scott could do it, though."

"That wasn't Randolph Scott in those old movies. That was a stunt man."

"I knew that," Rhodes said.

Ruth didn't reply. They were within twenty feet of Ferrin. She swung out of the road, bouncing the car over the ruts, and pulled alongside the ATV.

Ferrin looked over just as Rhodes opened the door. Rhodes hesitated just long enough to let Ferrin swing the ATV to his left. The front tire of the ATV struck the door and slammed it shut. Then Ferrin started to angle away from the car, out of the road and toward the trees.

"Try it again," Rhodes said, regretting his hesitation and determined not to be indecisive this time.

Ruth complied. The car bounced over the ruts in the opposite direction and pulled up beside Ferrin. This time Rhodes was ready. He threw the door open and jumped almost in the same motion.

Ferrin jerked the ATV to the right, but he wasn't quick

enough. Rhodes landed on him and knocked him loose from the handlebars, but both men remained atop the ATV, which swerved wildly to the right and left. Rhodes couldn't make much headway in subduing Ferrin. For the moment, it was all Rhodes could do just to hang on as the ATV slewed up the hill.

Ferrin grunted and jabbed a sharp elbow into Rhodes's ribs. Rhodes felt a stab of pain that made his head jerk backward.

He tried to tighten his arms around the writhing Ferrin, and looked to see where they were headed. What he saw didn't make him feel any better. What he saw was a tree just at the edge of the woods. He let go of Ferrin and threw himself aside just before the ATV hit the tree.

The sandy ground wasn't hard, but Rhodes rolled right through a mound of very angry fire ants, who were instantly on the attack, swarming onto his shoes and socks and crawling up his pant legs. He jumped up, slapping at his pants and hopping from one foot to another. Then his ankle gave way and he fell.

Ruth pulled up in the county car. She jumped out and drew her sidearm.

"He's getting away," she said.

Naturally, Rhodes thought, swatting at the ants, which were busily stinging him. Anybody else would have broken an arm or a leg, but Ferrin was apparently uninjured. And he was loose in the trees. At least he didn't have the ATV anymore.

Rhodes got up and said, "Let's go after him."

"Can you walk?"

"Sure," Rhodes said, though he wasn't sure at all.

It turned out that he could, if you wanted to call it walking. Hobbling was more like it. But he was more worried about the fire ants than about his ability to walk. He knew he was going to have blisters for days. He kept trying to smash them, but he knew he wasn't getting all of them.

"Come on," Ruth said, apparently not sympathetic with his plight.

Rhodes followed her, and they entered the woods beside the quiet ATV, which looked as if it had tried to climb the tree and had stopped only after its front tires left the ground.

Though the sun hadn't set, there was much less light by the time they got ten yards inside the woods. The sun had sunk a little below the hill, and its rays filtered only dimly into the trees.

Rhodes could hear Ferrin running along ahead of them. Ruth sprinted out after him, and Rhodes tried to keep up. He found that it didn't really make much difference to his ankle whether he walked or ran, so he kept running.

Dead leaves crackled beneath his feet and low branches whipped by his face. He put up a hand to keep them from swiping his eyes.

"He can't be too far ahead," Ruth said. "He's not going very fast."

Maybe he'd been hurt after all, Rhodes thought. Enough to slow him down, anyway. It seemed only fair.

"This way," Ruth said, turning to the right, where the trees didn't seem quite so thick.

Rhodes followed her after reaching down to scratch at his ant bites. He could still hear Ferrin up there ahead of them. Ferrin apparently wasn't much more of a woodsman than Rhodes was. If he kept making that much noise, he would be easy to track, but the farther they got into the trees, the darker it got.

Abruptly the noises in front of them came to a stop. Rhodes heard something flutter through the leaves over their heads, but that was all.

"Maybe he fell," Ruth said.

"Or maybe he's waiting for us," Rhodes said. "We have to be careful."

He was about to say more when a fire ant stung him

behind the knee. He rubbed his pants hard, hoping to squash the ant. He hoped none of them had gotten any higher. They were painful enough where they were. On the more delicate parts of the anatomy, they were pure torture.

Ruth went forward slowly. It was easier to walk than it had been, but the trees were still fairly close together. It would be easy for Ferrin to be lurking behind one.

Or *in* one, Rhodes thought, remembering Brother Alton. Rhodes drew his pistol and looked into the thick leaves. There was a dark shape in a tall bur oak tree not far from Ruth. It was obviously Ferrin.

"Hold on," Rhodes said to Ruth, who stopped and looked back. "He's up there."

Rhodes gestured with his pistol, and Ruth looked in the direction he indicated.

"Come on down, Ferrin," she said. "We've got you covered."

Rhodes thought it was a good line. Randolph Scott couldn't have said it any better.

Unfortunately, the dark shape didn't move. Maybe it wasn't Ferrin up there after all.

"I'm going to count to three," Ruth said. She didn't appear to have much doubt that Ferrin was in the tree. "If you're not down by then, I'm going to start shooting."

It was very still in the woods. Somewhere nearby a cricket started up.

"One," Ruth said.

She waited a beat. "Two."

She cocked her revolver. Rhodes could hear it from where he stood, but there was still no movement in the tree.

"Three."

Still no response.

Ruth pulled the trigger. A bullet ripped through the leaves and thudded into the trunk of the bur oak above Ferrin's head. The leaves trembled.

"Next one's in your leg," Ruth said.

"All right, I'm comin' down," Ferrin said.

The leaves rattled as he lowered himself to the bottom branch and then jumped to the ground. It wasn't far, only about a foot and a half.

Ruth had him put his hands on his head before she went up to him. She got him cuffed and marched him up to Rhodes.

"Let's put him in the car," Rhodes said. "It's time we were getting back to town."

17

▼

MICHAEL FERRIN REFUSED TO ADMIT THAT HE HAD KILLED Lige Ward. Oh, he admitted killing Rayjean, and he admitted that it had happened pretty much as Rhodes thought it had. But that was as far as he would go.

That worried Rhodes, but not because he'd been so sure that he was right. He'd been pretty sure, it was true, though he'd been leaning pretty heavily on a couple of inferences here and there. But what had worried him from the beginning was the fact that he had never been quite able to bring himself to believe that Ferrin had been sober enough to work out a plan as complicated as the one Rhodes attributed to him.

Ferrin admitted that Rhodes had guessed right about Ferrin's drive past Press Yardley's place. He even admitted having stopped there and talked to Ward.

"But that's all," he said. "I never killed him."

"You followed him back to his place, didn't you?" Rhodes asked.

"Okay, sure, I did that. We even had a little argument. He knocked me down a time or two, but that's all. I told him that I didn't have any money and that he could tell Wally Henry whatever he wanted to. Hell, what was Wally gonna do to me? Whip my ass, maybe, but that's all. He wouldn't kill me."

"And you didn't see anyone else at the cockpit, anyone that might've killed Lige?"

"Not a soul. Course all I wanted was to get out of there. I wasn't lookin' behind the trees."

Besides, Ferrin said, it hadn't been his idea at all to steal the outhouse. He had brought back the beer, and Larry and Kyle wanted to go riding around. Ferrin had driven them out to Obert, but they were the ones who insisted he turn down the road by King's; and they were the ones who wanted to steal the building. They thought it would be fun, and they were so emphatic that Ferrin, who wasn't as drunk as they were, hadn't seen any way to refuse. He found the pistol near the outhouse, but he didn't remember whose idea it had been to shoot holes in the portable building. It was fun; any of them might have thought of it.

Everything else had been pretty much the way Rhodes had reconstructed it. Lige had contended at the Palm Club that he didn't want to see Ferrin get hurt, but he had the evidence that Wally Henry had been cheated, and everyone knew that Wally didn't have much patience with cheaters. So Ferrin had grudgingly agreed to pay Lige off, though he really didn't intend to do it.

Ferrin had been looking for Lige's house when he spotted him at Yardley's. He'd driven out there because he was a little drunk, and he thought he might just do some damage to Lige's house or property in revenge for Lige's shakedown attempt. Seeing Lige taking the emus, Ferrin thought he might get off the hook by having something on Lige, so he stopped. They agreed to meet at the cockpit. Ferrin went, got shoved around, and left.

"I didn't shoot him," Ferrin insisted. "He was alive when I left there."

Rayjean Ward's death was something else again, and Ferrin regretted having caused it.

"I didn't mean to hurt her," he said. "She came runnin' down there all excited and wanted to know what I was doin'. I told her I was just lookin' for something, but she didn't believe me. She started yellin' and tryin' to hit me, so I hit her back. I didn't mean to hit her hard enough to kill her, but she was goin' wild. I just swung my hand to keep her off me. That's self-defense, right?"

"I'm not a lawyer," Rhodes said, scratching a fire-ant bite on the back of his leg.

"I guess I better get me one, then," Ferrin said, but he'd talked too much already.

Lige and Rayjean Ward were buried the next day in a little country cemetery not far from where they had lived most of their lives. It was in a quiet grove of cedar trees just off a dirt road, and it was surrounded by a wrought-iron fence that needed paint. No sounds from the highway reached there; the only noises were the trills of the birds and the wind in the cedars. There weren't many graves, not more than thirty, and a few of them dated back to the last century.

There was nothing new or modern about the place. It wasn't lighted at night, and there wasn't even a sign to call attention to it. The members of the cemetery association paid someone to keep the weeds cut and the grass mowed, but there was nothing they could do about the monuments, some of which were so old that the inscriptions were almost weathered away. Rhodes thought it was probably the kind of place where Ward would have wanted to be buried, a long way from discount centers and supermarkets.

There weren't many mourners, and most of those who were there were people who remembered the Wards from their days at the hardware store, old customers come to pay their last respects. Rhodes and Ivy were there because Rhodes thought he owed it to the Wards. He knew there was nothing he could have done to prevent the murders, but somehow he felt a sense of responsibility. Probably because of all that dog food he'd bought at Wal-Mart, he thought.

It was a hot day, but the shade of the cedars kept things from being too unpleasant. Still, Rhodes was uncomfortable because he was wearing an Ace bandage on his ankle, and the bandage was making him itch. He tried to ignore the itching and listen to the preacher.

Brother Alton conducted the funeral and led the hymns. The sunlight flashed off the lenses of his glasses as he spoke and sang. The songs were "We're Marching to Zion," which Rhodes liked because it didn't drag and because Brother Alton did the bass part on the chorus, and one about coming to the garden alone, which Rhodes could have done without. Much too slow.

Press Yardley and Nard King were there, too, though Rhodes noticed that they avoided standing anywhere near one another. As the mourners were leaving, Ivy went to speak to Rayjean's sister, while Rhodes walked over to Yardley, who was wiping his eyes with a handkerchief.

"I don't want to talk about this," Yardley said, folding his handkerchief and putting it back into the inside pocket of the dark suit coat he was wearing.

Rhodes wasn't surprised. "I know you don't, but I have to say a few things to you."

Yardley followed the sheriff over to the shade of a tall cedar and looked back at the graves.

"I know what Rayjean and I did was wrong," he said. "But it was Lige's fault. He never touched her after the store closed down."

"I thought you didn't want to talk about it," Rhodes said.

"You're right. I don't. What did you want to say to me?"

"It has to do with guineas," Rhodes told him.

"Guineas? Whose?"

"Lige's. The thing is, Michael Ferrin admits that he killed Rayjean, but not Lige. I've been thinking about that. Why admit one murder and not the other? It doesn't make sense, not if you were guilty of both of them."

"The talk is that he's going for self-defense on Rayjean's murder," Yardley said. "Maybe he didn't think he could get away with that on Lige."

"Maybe," Rhodes said. "But I was talking it over with Ivy last night, and she asked me something. She asked me why Rayjean didn't hear the guineas."

Yardley looked wary, but he kept his voice level. "When do you mean?"

"When Lige drove by the house the night he was killed. And when Ferrin followed him. Those guineas would've set up a clatter you could hear all the way to your house."

"So what? I don't see the problem."

Rhodes looked over at the other mourners. They were moving away from the grave now. Ivy was still talking to Rayjean's sister, and a few people were talking to Brother Alton, probably telling him what a nice funeral it had been. Ruth Grady was standing off to one side because Rhodes had asked her to come, just in case.

"I think you do see the problem," Rhodes told Yardley. "If a woman was worried about her husband coming home, she'd hear the guineas. If a man were somewhere that he wasn't supposed to be, he'd hear them, too. When Ivy and I left your house the day I came to check on your emus, she told me that you got really upset when she mentioned the guineas. You did hear them that night, didn't you?"

"Maybe. I don't remember."

"You remember all right. What if I were to tell you that Ferrin saw you walking down toward the cockpit that night?"

"He couldn't have. I—"

"He couldn't have? Because you hid when you saw his truck? How do you know he didn't stop and look back when he got to the road?"

If Yardley had been a hardened criminal, he might have pulled it off. He'd lied pretty well so far. But he was just an ordinary man who'd gotten into a situation he could no longer control. His shoulders slumped and he looked at the ground.

"That was quite a story you told me about the gun," Rhodes said. "It fooled me for a while, but you killed Lige, didn't you?"

"Yes," Yardley said, almost as if he were glad to get it off his chest. "I did."

He rode back to town with Ruth in the county car. Ivy drove Yardley's car, and Rhodes went back alone.

"I can't believe it," Hack said. "We had him dead to rights from the minute my computer told us who that gun belonged to, and you let him off the hook."

Lawton was on Rhodes's side, most likely because he was tired of hearing Hack brag about his electronic marvel. "Mr. Yardley said Lige took the pistol away from him, remember? How was anybody to know any different?"

"A lawman's supposed to know when somebody's lyin'," Hack said. "The sheriff tells us all the time how that's one thing that makes him different from the computer. Ain't that right, Sheriff? A computer can't tell if somebody's lyin', but a man can."

"Not always," Rhodes said. "And the story he told made him look so bad, I figured at first that it had to be the truth. When a man lies, he usually doesn't tell a story that puts him in such a bad light."

He didn't add that he had suspected Yardley's story from the beginning. He didn't think it would make any difference to Hack, and it probably wouldn't.

But the truth was that Yardley had never lost his gun to Lige at all. The confrontation Yardley had described had taken place, but Lige hadn't taken the gun from him. Yardley had never gotten it out of hiding that day. Instead he had denied everything to Lige. He swore that there was nothing going on between himself and Rayjean, and he had thought Lige was convinced.

Nevertheless, he'd taken the pistol along on his visit to Rayjean, just in case. When they'd heard the guineas, she asked him to go and investigate. He didn't see Lige's truck drive by, but he saw Ferrin's, though of course he didn't know to whom it belonged. Rayjean was scared that someone was after something or somebody, so Yardley had gotten dressed and started walking down to the cockpit.

"I walked off the road, so no one would see me if they left," he said. "Before I got there, the red truck drove back by, but I was lying in the weeds so the driver couldn't see me. When he was gone, I walked the rest of the way. Lige was there."

Yardley had tried to sneak away without being seen, but Lige heard him and caught up to him. They went back to the cockpit, with Yardley trying to explain what he was doing there and Lige adding two and two together.

"He was already mad," Yardley said. "You could see it in his eyes. And when he made up his mind that he'd been right all along about me and Rayjean, he was ready to kill me. I pulled out the pistol, and he tried to grab it. I guess I pulled the trigger."

Another self-defense plea, Rhodes thought, or maybe Yardley was trying to call it an accidental shooting. Involuntary manslaughter.

"What about hiding the body?" he asked.

"That was my idea," Yardley admitted. "I thought maybe Nard King would get the blame. He's new around here; nobody knows him. Maybe people would think he caught Lige fooling around his emu pens." Yardley gave a rueful laugh. "I went home and got my truck, put Lige in it and took him to the outhouse. I guess that's when I lost the pistol. It was stuck in my belt, and it probably fell out when I was wrestling Lige into the outhouse. I never noticed it was gone until the next day, and then it was too late to go back and look for it."

"So you didn't know that Lige had stolen your emus?"

"Not then," Yardley said. "I found that out the next day, too. Kind of ironic that Lige had been stealing from me while I was at his house with his wife."

"You weren't trying to implicate King because he was a thief, then?"

"No. But knowing what I know now, I wish he'd been blamed. It might've worked if those stupid kids hadn't stolen the outhouse."

Rhodes wasn't so sure about that, but stranger things had happened. What he wondered about now was why Yardley had reported his emus' being stolen. Why bother to call attention to himself that way?

"I had to carry on as if nothing had happened. What would King have thought if I hadn't reported the theft? He knew the emus were stolen. He had 'em. And if it hadn't been him, someone else would've known. So I had to report it. Otherwise, everyone would've been suspicious." He paused. "Do you think I'll ever get them back?"

"No," Rhodes said. "I don't think so."

Two days later, Rhodes was at the jail working on a report about a damaged electric gate. Someone driving down a county road had shot a hole through the control center, freezing the gate closed, and the owner wanted blood.

The telephone rang, and Hack answered.

"Sheriff's department," he said, and then listened for a minute. "Stolen emus, huh? Seems like there's a regular epidemic of that round here lately." He listened some more. "All right. I'll tell the sheriff, and he'll send somebody out there."

He started to hang up the phone, and Rhodes could hear a voice yelling on the other end. Hack put the phone back to his ear and listened.

Then he said, "Yessir, we'll get right on it. We won't keep you waitin'." He hung up and turned to Rhodes. "You wanta do this one? You can put off that report for a while."

That sounded like a good idea to Rhodes, except for the part about the emus. He'd had enough to do with stolen emus, not to mention roosters and guineas, to last him for a long time.

"Who was that?" he asked.

"That's the part you're gonna like," Hack said.

"Good. Tell me who it was, then."

"You don't wanta guess?"

"No," Rhodes said. "This is supposed to be a professional law-enforcement operation. I don't want to guess."

"You don't have to get huffy about it."

Rhodes took a deep breath. "I'm not getting huffy. Now, who was it?"

"Nard King," Hack said.

Rhodes looked at the emu pens. Some of the birds were still there. He asked how many were missing.

"Two," King said. "And what're you gonna do about it?" His face was red, as if his blood pressure was up quite a few points.

"Do you have the bills of sale?" Rhodes asked.

King exploded. "Hell no, I don't! I told you I didn't! What difference does that make?"

"If you don't have a bill of sale, you can't prove you owned those birds," Rhodes explained.

"You saw 'em! They were right out there in the pens!"

"I saw some emus. But to tell you the truth, I can't tell one from the other. How can I identify them?"

"Some sheriff you are!" King said. "Letting a man's emus get stolen right in front of your nose!"

"You're probably right about that," Rhodes said, knowing he'd surely lost a vote in the next election. "You ought to get a quieter air conditioner. Then maybe you could hear what was going on around here."

"What about that Yardley?" King asked. "They get his?"

Rhodes figured he knew what King was thinking, though maybe not. Maybe he was attributing unworthy thoughts to a worthy man. But he didn't think so.

"His cousin has a little place just outside Waco. He drove over and got them the day Press went to jail. So you won't find any emus there."

As a matter of fact, Rhodes wondered if that might not be exactly where the emus were. He'd told the cousin, whose name was George Yardley, all about the missing emus, and George had expressed a keen interest in the fact that King didn't have the bills of sale for the birds. He'd even asked what might happen if someone stole the emus from King.

"I wasn't thinkin' that I'd find my birds in Waco," King said.

"I hope not," Rhodes told him.

Before heading back to the jail, Rhodes drove over to the Ward place. The guineas scattered in front of his car, pot-tracking raucously, but otherwise the place was deserted.

Rhodes wondered if Rayjean's sister was going to keep the place up. Guineas could fend for themselves pretty well, but sooner or later they were going to need someone to feed them. He'd have to give the sister a call when he got back to town. If she wasn't willing to feed the guineas, Rhodes might have to drive out now and then to give them a little hen scratch.

After all, somebody had to take care of them.

5 A 577FRY
DU
09/96 1158-89   51 S.W.E